Frederic Edward Weatherly

Oxford days

or, How Ross got his degree

Frederic Edward Weatherly

Oxford days
or, How Ross got his degree

ISBN/EAN: 9783337712020

Printed in Europe, USA, Canada, Australia, Japan

Cover: Foto ©Andreas Hilbeck / pixelio.de

More available books at **www.hansebooks.com**

OXFORD DAYS;

or,

HOW ROSS GOT HIS DEGREE.

By A RESIDENT M.A.

London:

SAMPSON LOW, MARSTON, SEARLE, & RIVINGTON,

CROWN BUILDINGS, 188, FLEET STREET.

1879.

PREFACE.

———

" OXFORD DAYS " is not shaped on the lines of
either *Verdant Green* or *Tom Brown at Oxford*.
Its purpose, rather, is to furnish a practical guide
to all the features of University life ; but it has
been thought that, by adopting the narrative
form, the dry bones of a handbook may be made
to live.

Oxford, 1879.

CONTENTS.

OXFORD DAYS;

OR,

HOW ROSS GOT HIS DEGREE.

———◆———

CHAPTER I.

GONE TO OXFORD.

THERE was a long discussion between the Vicar of Porchester and Mr. Ross, the lawyer, as they walked together after evening service to the vicarage. Frank Ross was just eighteen, the eldest of six brothers. He was still at school, but it was time for him to go to the University. Oxford had been chosen—not from any notion of superiority to Cambridge, but simply because of school and home associations. The difficulty was the choice of a college. The vicar—a well-to-do bachelor—an old Eton and Christ-Church man, advised his own college. But Mr. Ross was frightened. "Christ-Church" to him had ever

B

been a terror, and meant waste of time and money, in the shape of cards, drink, and horse-flesh; and all the vicar's eloquence could not shake his unfounded prejudice. The result of the discussion was that Mr. Ross decided to write to a friend at Oxford, settled there as a " coach;" and also to Mr. Rickards, a country doctor, with a family larger even than his own. The doctor's answer was as follows :—

"DEAR ROSS,—My boy is going to Brasenose: at least, he goes up in May to try for a close scholarship. I can give you no advice, as I know nothing about the place. I sent him to the Hereford Cathedral School by a fluke some years ago; and as there are scholarships and exhibitions from the school to Brasenose, I am saved the difficulty of choosing a college.

"Yours truly,
"W. RICKARDS."

The vicar explained that a " close " scholarship was, like other scholarships, a sum of money paid annually for four or five years as a prize, but differed from them in being confined to competition among boys from certain schools; and that the value of them varied from 45*l.* to 80*l.* per annum, part being paid in money, and part made up in allowances in the way of diminished fees. The letter from the "coach" was more valuable:—

"DEAR MR. ROSS,—So much depends on your son's abilities, your own means and wishes, that I cannot answer your question as to the best college, off-hand. I think I may assume that you do not want him to spend more money than is absolutely necessary; and possibly that you would wish him to 'go in for honours' instead of taking a Pass Degree, that is, offering the smallest possible number of subjects for examination. I need hardly say that a high degree in honours opens the way to a Fellowship, or at any rate to good masterships in schools; and is, in fact, a distinct help, directly and indirectly, not only in educational, but in all professions.

"It is far better for a lad to go to a good college, even though he is unable to obtain a scholarship or any other college endowment, than to go to an inferior college, where he may succeed in getting pecuniary assistance. To illustrate what I mean: I believe, in the long run, it would be wiser to send your son as a commoner to Balliol than as a scholar to Wadham. If, from a pecuniary point of view, you do not care for him to get a scholarship, nor want him to read for honours, and are not particular as to whether he spends 300*l*. or 500*l*. a year (or even more), I should send him to Christ-Church, Brasenose, Exeter, or University. The first two especially were in my day emphatically popular colleges, and I believe are so still. But I would not send him to either unless you are fully prepared for the amount of expenditure which I have named. Possibly you might like our only denominational college—Keble. He would be most carefully looked after in every way, and his expenses kept within a fixed limit. The Warden and Tutors devote their whole energies to their men, and the men themselves speak in the most affectionate terms of them—a most exceptional fact, I assure you. But I must warn you that the religious tone of the college is distinctly pronounced, and inclines to ritualistic rather than to evangelical doctrines.

"If your son's college life will be a pinch to you (you will allow me to speak thus plainly on such a question), send him as an Unattached Student. But here, again, you and he should clearly understand that the life of an un-attached student is isolated, and quite unlike the life of the college undergraduate. The only exception to this state-ment is when an undergraduate migrates, as for various reasons sometimes he is obliged, from his college to the body of the Unattached. His society, being already formed, remains unbroken. I should fancy your choice will lie between New College, Corpus, Paul's, and Balliol. A scholarship at either means that the scholar is capable, with industry, of gaining the highest honours in his future University examinations. On the whole, I think, I incline to Paul's. Unfortunately, you have just missed the exami-nation for scholarships. There is, however, an ordinary matriculation examination for commoners in about three weeks' time. If your son holds a good position in his school, he ought to have no difficulty in passing even at this short notice, for the subjects are those which are read in forms lower than the highest at all schools. I shall be happy to do anything further in the matter for you that I can. He should come prepared for residence, in the event of his passing. The examination begins on the Wednesday after Easter, and will be over in time for successful candidates to 'come into residence' with the other men on the following

Saturday. You should send an application to the Master of Paul's at once. I enclose a list of subjects and fees, and am

"Yours truly,

"PHILIP WODEHOUSE."

"SUBJECTS FOR MATRICULATION AT PAUL'S.[1]

" 1. Translation from English into Latin prose.

" 2. Translation into English of an unprepared passage of Attic Greek.

" 3. Translation of some portion of a Greek and Latin author (to be selected by the candidate), with parsing and general grammar questions.

" 4. Arithmetic, including Vulgar and Decimal Fractions and Interest.

" 5. Euclid, Books I. and II.; *or* Algebra, to Simple Equations.

" FEES.

" (*a*) To the University at Matriculation .. 2*l*. 10*s*.

" (*b*) To the College, as caution-money .. 30*l*.[2]

"Room-rent varies from 10*l*. to 16*l*. per annum. This does not include furniture, which must be taken at a valuation from the previous tenant ; 25*l*. is an average valuation-price. China, glass, linen, plate, and household necessaries must all be procured. It is wiser to bring plate and linen. The

---

[1] The subjects at other colleges are much the same, but the standard of excellence required varies. No. 2 is usually omitted.

[2] At most colleges a reduction is made for scholars and exhibitioners.

rest may be purchased from the ' scout' (servant) apportioned
to the rooms. For this, say 10*l*. The immediate payments,
therefore, amount to 2*l*. 10*s*. + 30*l*. + 10*l*. = 42*l*. 10*s*.
The payment for the furniture must be made early in term ;
and the establishment charges, tuition fees, expenses of
board and rent, are paid terminally." [1]

So Paul's was chosen, and a letter of application forwarded to the Master; [2] and Frank, who
was then at home for the Easter vacation, commenced polishing up his work in view of the
approaching examination. On Easter Tuesday
he left home by an early train, with a note to
Mr. Wodehouse in his pocket. That gentleman
entertained him at dinner with a long list of
examination stories, and about nine o'clock
marched him off to the Clarendon Hotel, where,
with a word to the landlady, he left him, nervous
at the thought of the morrow, but conscious of
his own dignity and the near approach of the
manhood which is supposed to date from matriculation.

[1] At some colleges quarterly.

[2] The titles given to the different Heads of Colleges vary.
There is the Warden of New College, the Provost of Oriel,
the President of Trinity, the Master of Balliol, the Principal
of Brasenose, and the Rector of Exeter.

It was with some difficulty that Frank preserved
his self-composure in the presence of the waiters,
as he sat at breakfast in the " Clarendon " coffee-
room. He did not particularly enjoy his meal,
and, in obedience to Mr. Wodehouse's injunctions,
left at half-past nine to make his way to Paul's.
After one or two mistakes, he succeeded in finding
the college gates. His anxiety as to his next
step was set at rest by the sight that met him.
About a dozen boys (to be called men after
matriculation) were hanging about the Lodge, in
various typical conditions of mind and body—
some completely at their ease, chatting uncon-
cernedly; others standing nervously alone. Most
wore black coats and chimney-pot hats — the
costume that only a few years ago was rigorously
insisted on. A few through ignorance, or in
obedience to the spirit of the day, wore defiantly
light suits and bowler hats. Frank, to his great
delight, found a school-fellow whose coming up
had, like his own, been hurriedly decided in the
vacation. The two friends had not much time
for conversation, for in a few minutes a respect-
able middle-aged man, whom they knew afterwards to be the Porter, said, " You are to walk

this way, gentlemen, please," and conducted them
to the College-Hall. It is a fine old place, with
dark oak panels, coloured windows, portraits, and
coats-of-arms; and to the boy up in Oxford for
his first visit, and that visit so solemn a one as
matriculation, there is an unspeakable charm, and
a novelty sobered into grandeur, about everything.
How the grave faces of the college founders and
celebrities looked down upon the wondering eyes!
Bishop and knight, king and duchess—there
they stared! How the light streamed through
the coloured windows! Who could tell? Perhaps one day, Frank thought, when he was a
rich man, he might have that one vacant window filled, or some of his descendants might
present to the college a portrait of Sir Francis
Ross, attired in wig and gown, one of Her
Majesty's—or rather, perhaps, His Majesty's—
judges, if not Lord Chancellor.

He started abruptly from his dreams, and came
back to the first rung on the ladder that was
leading to such prospective fame. There before
him stretched three lines of tables and benches
down the length of the hall. Across the end, on
a slightly-raised daïs, ran another table, where

the handsome chairs indicated beings superior to undergraduates. It was, in fact, the High table, where the Master and Fellows dined, and any resident Masters of Arts who cared to do so.

This morning it was devoted to the more serious purposes of examination. Ten ink-bottles, fifteen blotting-bads, fifteen sheets of white paper printed, with a few sheets of blue paper and two or three quill pens lying by each : that was the fare this morning—" the feast of reason " that was in such strong contrast to the " flow of soul " that would grace the table at six o'clock that evening.

One of the junior Fellows was in charge of the examination. He was reading the *Times* as Frank and his companions entered, sitting on the table, with his legs dangling in a graceful attitude of studied negligence. He took no notice of the victims, till the Porter had conducted them to the table and motioned them to take seats. Then he looked up from his newspaper and said,—

" You will have till half-past twelve. Write your names clearly ; and please bear in mind that we expect answers from both books of Euclid."

Then he resumed his newspaper and adopted a more dignified attitude.

Frank looked at his questions. Eleven in all ; some definitions, six propositions from the first book, and four from the second. He wrote his name at the head of his paper, and made a great blot in doing so. His hand grew hot. He dashed at the first definition,—

"*A circle is a plane figure contained in one straight line.*"

His pen spluttered warningly at the word *straight.* A blot fell, and fell luckily on the fatal word. He tore up the paper and commenced again.

Making a good start, his hands grew cool, his head calm ; and with the old portraits beaming upon him, away he wrote. He completed the six propositions of the first book ; then, pausing for breath, saw that almost everybody else had his watch on the table. Frank pulled out his. *A quarter to twelve !* He had blundered, he knew. He ought to have timed himself, and left more time for the second book. However, his success had put him at his ease, for he knew all the propositions well so far; and he buckled-to vigorously.

By hard writing he managed to do three propositions. The last was the thirteenth. He knew
he could not do it in five minutes, and he must
allow himself time to read over his work. He
had barely done even this when the papers were
collected, and they were dismissed, with instructions to appear again at two.

Frank went out with his friend, discussing the
Euclid paper.

They lunched together at the " Clarendon,"
wisely confining themselves to a little cold meat
and sherry, and at two o'clock were again hard
at work at Latin prose. It was a piece from
" Pilgrim's Progress "—something about Giant
Despair, his wife, and her bed. And judging
from the various unhappy faces, an observer might
have thought that the choice of the giant was
somewhat prophetical. Frank, however, had
done, not the identical piece, but several pieces in
the same style before, and accordingly did not
find so much difficulty.

Out at four o'clock, they strolled down Oriel
Street, past Corpus, by Merton Church, and into
Christ-Church Broad Walk; and meeting three
friends, also up for matriculation at some other

college, took a boat from Salter's and rowed to Iffley, Frank steering.

Luckily the river was not crowded, as in full term, or the erratic course which Frank steered would have brought down upon him the shrill abuse of some eight-oar's coxswain, even if not a quiet spill into the water.

Thursday passed much in the same way: Frank, on the whole, satisfied with his work; Monkton, his friend, somewhat desponding. The hours after work would have been dull had there not been so much to see. The friends mooned about till half-past six, and then had meat-tea at Monkton's lodgings in Ship Street; and with "Verdant Green" and the "Mysteries of the Isis" beguiled the evening till they turned into bed. What a relief it was when Friday morning came, and with it the last paper! At two that afternoon they were met in the Lodge by the Porter, who had an important-looking paper in his hands.

"Please to wait a moment, gentlemen," he said, as all the candidates were hurrying off across the quadrangle to the hall; "these are the gentlemen that are to go for *vivâ voce.*" And he proceeded to read out six names, among which Frank and

Monkton, to their great delight, heard their own.
They hardly thought of the disconsolate nine who,
hearing the last name on the list, hopelessly
oozed one by one out at the Lodge-gates.

Reaching the hall, the chosen six found the
Master and six of the Fellows, all attired in cap,
gown, and dignity, seated at the High table.
They were told to sit down at one side of the hall,
and then, one by one, were summoned to that
awful table and examined. Monkton's ordeal
came first, and it was a trying one. He was first
questioned (very sharply, as it seemed to Frank)
on some of his papers, and then given some written
questions and sent to a side table. Frank was
not aware, then, that this process—familiarly
known as "second paper"—meant that Monkton's success hung by a thread on the result of
his work this afternoon. His own turn came
next. The Fellow who examined him saw he was
nervous, and, as usual with almost every examiner,
spoke pleasantly and reassuringly to him.

"Take your Greek Testament, Mr. Ross," he
said, "and turn to the fifth chapter of St. Matthew,
and translate the first six verses."

Frank turned to the passage indicated. He

knew it at a glance, and that reassured him ; and when he was next told to open a " Cicero " that was lying on the table he felt comparatively at his ease. He got through about six lines of the Second Philippic, and was then asked a few disconnected questions.

" Do you know what circumstances led to the delivery of this speech ?"

He did know, but words failed him, and he bungled.

"Never mind," answered the examiner. " Who was Hannibal ? and what battles did he fight ?"

Frank answered, naming them.

" What is the construction after verbs of commanding in Latin ?"

" Can you mention any of our Lord's parables which teach the duty of watchfulness ?" and so forth.

Then came the pleasant dismissal,—

" That will do, thank you. You need not wait."

Frank departed, and, making friends with the Porter, told him all that had passed.

" Ah ! you're all right, sir," said George ; and George's statement proved true.

In about three-quarters of an hour the Master and Fellows came out of the hall and dispersed to their respective rooms, and presently George appeared with a piece of blue paper, which he nailed on the gate. Five names—Frank's second, and Monkton's absent.

"Those gentlemen that mean to reside this term," said George, "are to call on the Dean between five and six this evening, and bring their fees. Those that don't are to leave Oxford at once, and notice will be sent to them in the Long Vacation before next term begins."

Frank meant to reside, and was one of the first to call on the Dean. That gentleman received him courteously; told him he had done very fairly in the examination; hoped he would read hard and be steady; asked him his name, age, father's name, residence, and profession, and various other particulars, all of which he entered in a book; received his caution-money (30*l.*), and told him to ask the Porter the staircase and number of the rooms allotted to him.

"Be here," he added, as Frank was leaving, "at a quarter to ten to-morrow morning, that I may take you before the Vice-Chancellor."

At the Porter's advice, Frank took a cab and drove to the "Clarendon," paid his bill, got his luggage together, and drove back to college. By this time the Porter had the list of the newly-allotted rooms.

"Yours are No. 5, sir, three-pair right."

Frank stared.

"No. 5 over the doorway, sir," he then explained, pointing across the quadrangle to a doorway, over which Frank discerned the wished-for number; "three flights o' stairs; the rooms on the right hand. No. 5, three-pair right—that's how we call it. You'll find your scout there. You're too late for dinner. The hall-bell went twenty minutes ago."

Frank crossed the quadrangle, climbed the stairs, and found his rooms. They were neither large, nor particularly clean, as regarded paper and paint; and the carpets and coverings were decidedly dingy. But they were *his* rooms, and he was an Oxford man! and that was *his* scout bustling in from the rooms opposite to welcome him. After a little conversation, the fact of his ownership became still more apparent, for the scout proceeded to show him a collection of glass

and china and household implements, on the
merits and absolute necessity of which he enlarged.
The mere transfer of glass and china supplies a
nice little addition to the scout's perquisites.
The articles are, in the first instance, purchased
by some undergraduate who prefers his own
choice to what his scout has ready to offer him.
He, on leaving his rooms, bequeaths them to
his scout. Custom is so tyrannical in Oxford.
The scout sells the articles to the next tenant,
who, in his turn, bequeaths them to the same
willing legatee, when again they are sold to
the new-comer. How long this goes on it is
hard to say. Sometimes the smooth course
is interrupted by some strong-minded undergraduate, who, ignoring custom, takes his effects
with him when he leaves. The little bill was as
follows :—

FRANK ROSS, ESQ., *to* WILLIAM GREEN.

	£	s.	d.
3 Cut-glass Decanters	2	0	0
Claret Jug	1	0	0
3 dozen Wine-glasses (mixed) . .	1	10	0
8 Tumblers	0	9	6
A Dessert Set	0	18	0
15 Dinner Plates	0	13	6

7 Cheese Plates	0	5	6
Tea Set, consisting of Milk Jug, Sugar Basin, Bowl, 8 Breakfast Cups, 6 Tea Cups, 9 Plates (all mixed) .	2	2	0
Metal Tea-pot	0	7	6
Broom	0	8	0
Dustpan and Brush	0	3	6
6 Dusters	0	6	0
6 Tea-cloths	0	6	0

£9 19 6

Shortly afterwards, as Frank was unpacking, a youth of most obsequious manners arrived, carrying a cap and gown for the Freshman, who received them with a murmur of gratified pleasure, making no inquiries about the cost or who had given the order; considering that, of course, what was thus sent must be *en règle.* The bill arrived within a week, with a polite intimation that payment was not requested, and an invitation to inspect the stock of the obliging tailors.

FRANK ROSS, ESQ., *to* CUTTER AND CO.

	s.	*d.*
A College Cap	7	6
A Commoner's Gown . . .	15	0

£1 2 6

Three years later, when pressed by duns and threatened with proceedings in the Vice-Chancellor's Court, Frank remembered these gentle disclaimers of any wish for payment.

What with talking to his scout and unpacking, nine o'clock soon arrived: the hour when the kitchen and buttery were opened for supper. William suggested that his master would like some supper, and in a short time supper was brought.

"I shan't eat all that," expostulated Frank, when he saw the plateful of meat and lumps of bread and butter.

"Only one 'commons,' sir," replied William.

Frank said nothing, but saw distinctly that the standard called "one commons," for which his father would have to pay daily through his three or four years, was based on the principle that "what is ordered for one should be enough for two." However, he enjoyed his supper; and so did the scout, who carried home his share, with similar portions from the other six rooms on the staircase to which it was his duty to attend.

The following morning, duly attired in cap and gown, with white tie and black coat at William's suggestion, Frank betook himself to the Dean's rooms. There he met the four other Freshmen who had " passed " with him, was asked if he had his fee ready, and then conducted in a sheepish, silent procession, headed by the Dean, to the Vice-Chancellor. There were several groups of Freshmen standing with their respective Deans, Vice-Principals, or other college officials. Then they were all told to write their names in a book in Latin—a novel though not difficult feat, which Frank, with the assistance of his Dean, accomplished.

" Ross, Franciscus, filius Armigeri, è collegio S. Pauli."

He then handed in his fee, 2*l.* 10*s.*, and received in return a little piece of blue paper, the certificate of matriculation, together with a copy of the University statutes. The Vice-Chancellor addressed them all in a short Latin formula; and when this was over, Frank had time to read the document, which ran thus :—

" Term. Pasch.

" Oxoniæ, die Ap. 27mo, Anno Domini 187—.

" Quo die comparuit coram me Franciscus Ross, è Coll. S. Pauli, Arm. Fil. et admonitus est de observandis statutis hujus Universitatis et in matriculam Universitatis relatus est.

" ——, Vice-Can."

He was now fully matriculated, and amenable to all the details of University discipline. At six o'clock he dined in Hall—his first dinner—not without the usual blunder of seating himself at a table appropriated to undergraduates at least two years his seniors; and at eight went to chapel—the hour being changed on first nights in term from half-past five to eight, to enable men from distant homes to put in an appearance. The chapel was very much crowded, Paul's having considerably outgrown its accommodation; but it was only on first nights that the inconvenience was felt, for as it was not necessary to attend service more than four times in the week, all the men were never there together.

Coming out, he met several old school-fellows, and the senior of them carried them all off to his lodgings in Holywell Street, where over wine and pipes they sat chatting till past ten o'clock; Frank, for the most part, listening without saying much, for he was but a Freshman, and this his first pipe.

When he got back to Paul's he found the gates locked; but as he had read " Verdant Green " very carefully, he did not think it necessary to apologize to George for giving him the trouble of opening. He knew that "knocking in" before eleven o'clock only meant twopence in his weekly "battels." [1]

That night, when he got into bed, though he did not feel quite a "man," he felt conscious of having undergone some considerable change since he left home on Tuesday morning.

[1] College bills.

CHAPTER II.

AN OXFORD SUNDAY.

ON Sunday morning he woke to the words that, without the slightest variation in time or tone of delivery, called him daily for the three years that he resided in college—"Half-past seven, sir! Do you breakfast in ? "

This was the scout's gentle hint that chapel service was within half an hour, and his form of inquiry whether his young master intended breakfasting in his own rooms or was going elsewhere for the meal.

Frank, when he fully realized the meaning, answered "Yes," and with a freshman's energy jumped out of bed, and was dressed before the chapel bell began to ring. Hurrying downstairs, in fear of being late, he was stopped by William, with the suggestion that there was "no call to go yet, till the bell began to swear ! "

This elegant expression, Frank learnt, is applied to the quickened and louder ringing of the bell for the five minutes immediately preceding service. He found, not many days after, that it was quite possible, by the aid of an Ulster, and postponement of ablutions, to get to chapel in time if he slept till the "swearing" began.

There were not so many men present as on the previous evening. The Master and Fellows wore surplices and hoods; the Scholars, being undergraduates, surplices and no hoods; the commoners, black gowns. The few—apparently senior men—who wore black gowns of longer and ampler make than the commoners, were the Bachelors and Masters of Arts, still "in residence," but not on the foundation—*i. e.*, neither Fellows nor Scholars, and therefore not entitled to wear surplices. This was the strict order for Sundays, and other high days; on other days every one wore the black gown of his respective degree, with the single exception of the Fellow who did chaplain's duty for the week; for at Paul's there was no permanent chaplain. The first lesson was read by one of the Scholars, the second by one of the Fellows, the prayers by the chaplain, the Communion Service by the Master. There was no sermon; the intention being that each undergraduate should attend "prayers" in his own particular college-chapel, and afterwards hear a sermon preached in the University-church to the members of the University in common. The list of those who attend chapel is kept at Paul's by the Bible-clerk, at some colleges by the chapel-porter. The Bible-clerk's further duties are to find the lessons, to read them in the possible absence of the proper person, and to say grace in Hall.

A man may lose caste by becoming a Bible-clerk, but it is by no means necessary that he should. A cad (and there are many at Oxford) distinctly degrades the post, and makes it shunned. A man wavering between good sets and bad sets may possibly lose what little footing he has in the former. But a thorough gentleman (it seems hardly necessary to say so, except to disabuse many of their prejudices) need not, and does not in the slightest degree, lower himself by holding such a position. The emoluments amount (in money and allowances) often to 80*l*.

per annum; at Paul's, 75*l.*; but what makes the post so especially valuable, from a pecuniary point of view, is that it can be held with a Scholarship and an Exhibition. The Bible-clerk at Paul's during Frank's first two years was holding a Scholarship of the value of 60*l.*, an Exhibition from his school of the value of 50*l.*; so that, with his clerkship of 75*l.*, his income amounted to 185*l.*, for the academical year of six months. And he was one of the most popular men in the college.

From him Frank learnt that he would have to read the first lesson in chapel for six consecutive days in his turn; but that, being a freshman, his turn would not come for some time yet.

On returning to his rooms he found his breakfast laid, the kettle simmering, and letters lying on the table; one from home; the rest, the circulars that flatter the freshman's dignity, and coax him into becoming a customer.

The foundation breakfast consists of bread, butter, and milk, and in some colleges two eggs. These articles are brought by the scouts from the buttery, and entered by the buttery-clerk to the respective undergraduates. The bread, butter, and milk are distributed in "commons," the rate charged being above that of tradesmen outside college, and the quantity being, in the case of most men, certainly too much for one meal. The remains belong to the scout.

Fish, poultry, meat (and for luncheon, pastry), are supplied from the kitchen. For some items the charges are reasonable, for others exorbitant. Naturally, therefore, it is in "kitchen-orders" that the careful student can economize, if only he can stand against the Oxford custom, fostered by the scouts, of ordering too much. For at least three days in the week the two customary eggs, with bread and butter, are surely enough for breakfast, a kitchen-order being thereby avoided. The too common habit, however, is to discard the eggs (paid for, it must be remembered, whether eaten or not), and eat meat. It is quite conceivable that, after one breakfast on one staircase where eight men live, the scout may put into his basket sixteen eggs.

Tea, coffee, chocolate, cocoa, sugar, and so on, are in some colleges procurable from the Common-room-stores, an establishment resembling an Italian warehouse and wine-and-spirit-vault combined.   Custom, if not college regulations, will compel the undergraduate to deal with the Common-room-man.

At Paul's there is no such establishment, but William very kindly supplied the deficiency by ordering in, from one of the nearest—and dearest —grocers, a good stock of tea (at 4s. 6d. per pound, of course), coffee, candles, matches, scented soap, biscuits, jam, marmalade, till Frank was quite bewildered at the thought of the room necessary for storing these delicacies.   However, they did not last long.

One of the most iniquitous and yet plausible practices is that pursued at some colleges—Paul's among the number—of compelling undergraduates to deal at certain shops.

Anything in the way of paper, paint, or furni-ture, has to be procured at one of the shops attached to the college.   These are invariably the dearest, charging for their goods 25 and 30 per cent. more than the many other establishments which struggle against these monopolies.

The reason given by the college authorities for this system is that they are obliged to exercise some principle of selection of the workmen allowed within the college walls, indiscriminate admission being open to risk. The reason is plausible enough, but it is based entirely on the supposition that the workmen employed by expensive firms alone are honest. Further, what risk could there be in the conveyance of a piece of furniture to the college gates, when its removal to the rooms of the purchaser would be the work of the college servants ?

The only method of avoiding the tyranny of the system is to employ one of the railway carriers. The college porter, on the presumption that the article has come by rail from the undergraduate's home, is obliged to admit it.

Anything like opposition to the regulation appears at present to be useless. One daring undergraduate at Paul's, who ventured to remonstrate with his college dean (the authority in such matters), was met with this characteristic answer :—" It is our system. If you don't like it, the college gates are open. You can remove your name from the college books. We won't detain you." — an answer perfectly admissible from the proprietor of any establishment, but insolent and unwarrantable from one who, after all, is but an administrator in a corporate institution.

And so it would be possible to go on and enumerate many instances in which not only custom among his companions, but college regulations compel the undergraduate to be extravagant and wasteful. Homes are crippled, younger brothers and sisters deprived of the education which is their due, and the much-vaunted University extension limited by the very administration of the bodies that ought, and do profess, to foster it. Questions of domestic economy are ignored by the various commissions, though they lie at the very root of University extension. Let additional Scholarships be founded to enable more students to come to the University; let additional teaching power be endowed with professorships, lectureships, and readerships, by all means; but let perquisites be pruned down; let the enormous profits of catering cooks and butlers be decreased; let room-rent be lowered; let "servants' dues" pay the servants, and not need to be supplemented by charges which never appear in the college accounts; let trade be free in the town; let every man buy where he pleases; that is the way to extend the benefits of University education—that is the way to enable those to profit by it who are at present debarred—that is the way to enable families, which now struggle to send one son to the University, to send two for an equivalent outlay. There can be no doubt of the unnecessary waste and extravagance in the domestic economy of the colleges when it is remembered that though collegiate life, based as it is on communistic principles, ought to be cheaper than any other form of student life, as a matter of fact it is considerably more expensive.

To return to Frank's breakfast. He found some difficulty in boiling his eggs and making his tea. But he concealed his ignorance and ate the eggs, and drank his tea like dish-water.

About a quarter to ten some one banged at his door, and entered with the bang. The visitor was Crawford, of Brasenose, an old school-fellow of Frank's, who had gone up about three years previously.

"Hullo, young man! not finished breakfast yet!"

His cheery greeting was delightful to Frank, who felt he had in him a true friend.

A man about three years senior to a freshman
—what a power, for good or evil, he has ! His
seniority inspires reverence and commands imitation. Luckily, Crawford was a thoroughly ster-
ling fellow. He had come to Oxford in earnest.
When he worked he worked ; when he played he
played. There was the same vigour in his work
as in his " stroke " on the river or " rush " at
football. He kept chapels regularly ; he said,
because morning-chapel gave him a long day.
There was a more earnest reason concealed behind
this ; but he had a horror of the dangers of cant.
He knew what lectures were worth attending, and
attended them. He ridiculed and cut the worth-
less. He knew who were the best " coaches," and
said so. He abused the charlatans. In all matters
of social etiquette he was an old-fashioned Conservative ; for example, he always wore a black coat
and tall hat on Sundays, and roundly abused those
who loafed in light suits ; and he never carried an
umbrella or wore gloves when attired in cap and
gown—a rather silly custom, perhaps ; but its ob-
servance in the face of innovations marks the man.

After a little chat on school matters, Crawford
told Frank he was going to the University

sermon; and without any compunction told him—not asked him—to accompany him.

Frank, nothing loth, took his cap and gown, and they went together.

St. Mary's does double duty: as a parish church and as the University church; and here the University sermons are preached at 10.30 a.m. and 2 p.m. on each Sunday in full term, except those of the Dean of Christ-Church, or the Fellows of New College, Magdalen, and Merton, which are or may be preached in the cathedral and in the chapels of those colleges respectively.

The nave—the part appropriated to the University—was crowded when Frank and his companion entered, for the preacher was a popular one. In the gallery, facing that by the west window assigned to undergraduates, the University organist, Mr. Taylor, was already seated at the organ, with six or eight chorister boys round him. One of these hung a board, with the number of the selected hymn, over the gallery, and then the voluntary commenced.

At 10.30 precisely the procession entered at the north door: the vice-chancellor, preceded by his mace-bearers, the esquire bedels and marshals, and followed by the heads of houses, the preacher, and the proctors. Then the whole congregation rose and, led by the choristers, sang the hymn appointed. Afterwards came the quaint " bidding prayer," still used in most cathedrals, but made especially quaint in a University city by the long lists of founders and benefactors; and then the sermon. At a quarter to twelve all was over, and Frank was sitting in the window of Crawford's rooms in Brasenose; and as he looked out on the sunny Radcliffe Square, with St. Mary's graceful spire, the black frowning " schools," and the pepper-box towers of All Souls, he heard with reverent admiration (for he was, in his way, somewhat of a poet) that these were Bishop Heber's rooms, that here he must have sat, and here he must have written that famous Newdigate prize-poem, " Palestine," by which he will always be remembered.

Over the chimney looking-glass hung a gilded face, with an enormous nose, the emblem of the college. The pictures on the panelled walls Frank soon became more intimately acquainted with, for he found copies in most of his friends' rooms. There were " The Huguenots," " The

Black Brunswicker," Landseer's "Challenge,"
" Retreat," and " Monarch of the Glen," of course,
and many others of a more recent date. Three or
four pairs of boxing-gloves lay in one corner,
dumb-bells in another. Against the wall, in
racks, pipes of various descriptions, from the
short briar-root to the china bowl of the German
student (for Crawford had spent six months once
upon a time in Heidelberg), racket-bats, and an
oar, fondly cherished, that had helped to bring
victory to the Brasenose " four " a few years back
at Henley.

At one o'clock Crawford's scout appeared, and
almost at the same moment three invited friends,
strangers to Frank. At Oxford luncheon or
breakfast parties, etiquette does not require that
the guests should arrive late. The lunch was as
follows :—

Leg of lamb.	Celery.
Couple of chicken.	Three pots of jam.
Ham cut in huge slices.	" French pastry " (in
Salad.	reality, English
Lumps of bread.	tarts).
Lumps of butter.	Cyder cup.
Lumps of cheese.	Sherry and claret.

Fish, meat, and marmalade at nine that morning, and a prospective dinner in Hall at six that evening, did not prevent Frank's four companions from doing ample justice to the fare. He himself was as yet unused to these meals, by which circumstance Crawford's scout profited.

After lunch, pipes. At three the guests dropped off; and the two school-fellows walked to Cumnor—as a result of which Frank wasted three hours on Monday evening, writing a poem about Amy Robsart's tomb.

At five they got back to Oxford, and the freshman was introduced to the reading and writing rooms of the Union Society, Crawford entering his name as a probationary member, and telling him to call on Monday to pay the fee—25*s*. There was hardly time to do more than glance at the telegrams in the hall, and just look in at the numerous readers and writers in the different rooms; but the view was quite enough to enchant Frank. And then the friends parted for their respective chapels.

At dinner that evening he made friends with some freshmen, with one of whom he proposed to go to St. Philip's and St. James' Church, for evening service. Dinner being prolonged rather beyond the usual time, they had to run pretty sharp, and even then were too late to get a seat. They accordingly began to retrace their steps, determining on future occasions, when they meant to go to either of the parish churches, to make their dinner at lunch-time, and " take their names off Hall "—i.e. remove their names from the list of those for whom dinner in Hall was provided—and have supper in their rooms on their return from service.

As they were walking on, they were suddenly stopped by a man having the appearance of a policeman in plain clothes, who said,—

" The Proctor wants to speak to you, gentlemen."

The next moment they saw a gentleman in black gown and large velvet sleeves, who with formal politeness raised his cap and said,—

" Are you members of this University ? "

Frank and his friend murmured that they were.

" Your names and colleges, if you please."

" Ross of Paul's."

" Mordaunt, of Paul's."

" Call on me to-morrow morning at nine, if you please."

And the Proctor walked on, leaving Frank and Mordaunt rather bewildered, and totally ignorant where they were to call in the morning—for though they knew they had been "proctorized," they did not know either the Proctor's name or his college.

The marshal (the Proctor's head attendant; the rest being called "bull-dogs"), seeing them standing in the road in evident uncertainty, said to them,—

"You'd best go back to college, gentlemen;" and then, instinctively gathering that they were freshmen, added,—

"Where's your caps and gowns? You'll find the Proctor at Christ-Church, gentlemen," and vanished with his bull-dogs after other unwary undergraduates.

The interview somewhat damped their spirits : not that any fearful punishment was hanging over their heads. Even the statutable fine of five shillings for being without cap and gown would, they believed, be remitted in consideration of their being freshmen. But Frank had hoped to keep out of the way of the Proctors; and this was indeed an early beginning.

CHAPTER III.

THE FRESHMAN'S TERM.

STROLLING towards the Lodge on Monday morning—because everybody seemed to be strolling
in that direction—Frank had his attention called
to various notices posted in the gates. One was
to the effect that "the Master would see the gentlemen that morning between 10 a.m. and noon,
the freshmen on Tuesday, between the same
hours." Another that "the Dean would be glad
to see the freshmen at ten, the other gentlemen
after." There was also a list of places in Hall;
announcements of the meetings of the College
Debating Society, Boat Club, Cricket Club;
Greek Testament Lecture, *sine ulla solemnitate*
(i.e. without cap and gown), at Mr. Wood's house
every Sunday evening at nine. He was one of the
married Fellows—a hard-working, energetic man.

Without quite knowing what "seeing the

freshmen" meant, Frank got his gown, and as it was five minutes to ten, made his way to the Dean's rooms. In the passage outside he found about twenty freshmen cooling their heels, and engaged, some more and some less, in questions or chaff with George, the Dean's scout. George usually had the best of it. In fact, the freshman who dared to argue with him on matters of custom or local politics, and especially local politics, found himself considerably " shut up."

A door opened, and a sort of snort from within indicated to George that the Dean was ready to see the freshmen. One by one they filed in, and were greeted by the Dean with a smile that was naturally faint but tried to be sweet, and a grasp of the hand that was meant to be cordial but was unmistakably flabby. There were seats for all, but it took some minutes to get into them. The interview did not last long : just long enough, in fact, to enable the Dean to make one remark to each of the freshmen. To one, without waiting for an answer, " How is your father ? " To another, " Does Mr. St. Leger intend coming forward for Slowcombe ? " To another, " Have you been in Devonshire this vacation, Mr Jones ? "—

Jones being, of course, a Yorkshireman who has never travelled further south than Oxford, when he matriculated in February last. To one or two a faint question as to their intentions. "Were they going to read for Honours, or for a Pass?" On the whole, Frank left the room depressed and disheartened as to his work. He had expected to be questioned as to what he had done at school: what form he was in: what books he had read; to be advised as to the turn his reading should now take; whether he should read for Honours in one examination or in more than one; or whether, in short, reading for Honours would be beyond him, and therefore waste of time. The only piece of practical information he gained was that Mr. Wood was his tutor, and to him he must apply for all particulars as to Lectures and Examinations.

The plan at Paul's is similar to that at most colleges. The undergraduates are distributed among the tutors, a certain number being apportioned to each. They are not necessarily to attend their lectures, but they are to go to them for advice and private assistance in their work. In many colleges, battels are paid by the undergraduate to his own tutor. The tutors together draw up a scheme of lectures, which the undergraduates attend simply according to the necessities of the examination for which they are reading, and not according to the particular tutor to whom they are assigned. · Frank was assigned to Mr. Wood, but did not attend his Lectures in his first term, as they were for more advanced men. He learnt all this when he went to him at the Dean's direction. What he failed to find in the Dean he found in Mr. Wood, who met him cordially, took him into his inner room, made him sit comfortably on a sofa in the large bay window, and then chatted with him for half an hour. The result of the conversation was that Frank was to work for Responsions,[1] which would come

[1] Responsions are obligatory on all except those who have passed either the Previous Examination at Cambridge, or the Oxford and Cambridge Schools' Examination. There are five separate subjects of examination, in each of which a candidate must satisfy the Examiners (who, in this case, are called "Masters of the Schools"). The principle of compensation is not recognized ; failure in any one subject rendering a candidate liable to a "pluck" (commonly called "plough"). Subjects :—(1) Algebra : Addition, Subtraction, Multiplication, Division, Greatest Common Measure, Least Common Multiple, Fractions, Extraction of Square Root, Simple

on at the end of the current term; not to

Equations containing one or two unknown quantities, and problems producing such Equations; or Geometry—such an amount as shall be equivalent to that which is contained in Euclid I., II. (2) Arithmetic—the whole. (3) Latin and Greek Grammar. (4) Translation from English into Latin prose; it is sufficient if the Latin be grammatically written, without being elegant in style; three or four violations of the simple rules of Latin Syntax (commonly called " howlers ") will "plough" a candidate. (5) One Greek and one Latin Author; candidates are free to offer any standard classical authors, but the selection is usually made from the following list:—Homer: any five consecutive books; Æschylus: any two of the following plays—Agamemnon, Choephorœ, Eumenides, Prometheus Vinctus, Septem contra Thebas. Sophocles: any two plays. Euripides: any two of the following—Hecuba, Medea, Alcestis, Orestes, Phœnissœ, Hippolytus, Bacchœ. Aristophanes: any two of the following —Nubes, Ranœ, Acharnenses. Thucydides: any two consecutive books. Xenophon: Anabasis, any four consecutive books. Æschines: In Ctesiphontem. Virgil: (1) the Bucolics, with any three consecutive books of the Æneid; or (2) the Georgics; or (3) any five consecutive books of the Æneid. Horace: (1) any three books of the Odes, together with a book of the Satires, or of the Epistles, or the Ars Poetica; or (2) the Satires with the Ars Poetica; or (3) the Epistles with the Ars Poetica. Juvenal: the whole except Satires II., VI., IX. Livy: any two consecutive books, taken either from Books I.—V., or Books XXI.—XXV. Cæsar: De Bello Gallico, any four consecutive books. Sallust: Bellum Catilinarium, and Jugurthinum. Cicero: (1) the think about Moderations [1] till he was safe through this first ordeal; and to come on Sunday evenings to Mr. Wood's Greek Testament Lectures. The hours and subjects of the other lectures, he told Frank, he would find posted on the Lodge-gate on the following day. He asked him a few questions about his father and the Vicar of Porchester, who was an old friend; about his school and college friends; asked him whether he boated or played cricket; whether he meant to join the Union; told him if he wanted any books out of the college library to come to him; concluding hurriedly, as another freshman, seeking advice, knocked timorously and entered.

The visit next morning to the Master was not unlike that to the Dean—a purely formal one. The Master's questions chiefly related to cricket and boating, indicating an anxiety to discover the

first three Philippics; or (2) De Senectute and De Amicitia; or (3) four Catiline orations, with the oration Pro Archia. The books most commonly chosen are Euripides,—Hecuba, and Alcestis; and one of the combinations in Virgil or Horace.

[1] Moderations or First Public Examination will be explained in due course.

promising men for the Eleven or the Boats. Frank, as he sat in the Master's arm-chair, while the old gentleman warmed his coat-tails by an imaginary fire, could not help falling to making doggrel—

"'D' stands for Discipline, Duty, and Dean;
"'M' must the Master and Merriment mean."

But there he stopped by lack of rhymes and a general stampede of the Freshmen, to the great relief of the much-enduring Master.

Frank selected for Responsions the books he had offered for Matriculation, the usual and natural course; and with the assistance of Crawford to interpret the Lecture-List on the college gates, he made out his own lecture-card as follows:—

	9.	10.	11.	12.
Monday			Greek Plays —Mr. Lang	Latin Prose in Hall.
Tuesday		Cicero—Mr. Henderson		Grammar Paper.
Wednesday.			Greek Plays —Mr. Lang	Latin Prose in Hall.
Thursday ...	Prose to Mr. Wood	Cicero—Mr. Henderson		Grammar Paper.
Friday			Greek Plays —Mr. Lang	Latin Prose in Hall.
Saturday ...		Cicero—Mr. Henderson		Grammar Paper.

The lectures in his books were much the same
as at school, except that the undergraduates
were treated with more respect than school-boys.
A certain quantity was set: the men were put
on in turn to translate; and general questions
asked. Sometimes, if time permitted, the lecturer
would translate the lesson himself when the men
had finished.

The grammar and prose in Hall were in the
form of examination. The men were called up
one by one to be shown the mistakes in the
papers done on previous days, so that, with this
interruption, not much more than forty minutes
were left for actual writing. The prose on
Thursday morning was the only tutorial link
that bound Mr. Wood to his pupil, and that was,
as often as not, severed by a note to the effect
that Mr. Wood would be "unable to see Mr.
Ross on Thursday morning."

To Frank the work seemed as nothing after the
long hours of school. It never occurred to him
to look ahead, and to think of Moderations; in
fact, he had been told not to do so. And so he
commenced, energetically it is true, going over
work he already knew well enough to satisfy the

examiners, listening to the marvellous mistakes
of his fellow-freshmen and of those senior men
who had been degraded because of failure in
previous terms. He soon learnt to think nothing
of hearing mistakes that would disgrace school-
boys of fifteen; and to fancy that, because he
regularly prepared his work and attended his
lectures, he was working to the utmost extent
that he could, or that was required of him. And
that is how so many first terms are wasted, and
boys with energy enough for eight or ten hours'
daily study drift into two or three, and often
into none at all. Failure sometimes rouses them;
but it is a questionable remedy, and more often
demoralizes than benefits.

There is not much work done in the summer
term; an outsider might say, none at all. But
then he would be judging from the external
appearance of the place: the quads crowded with
lounging men, waiting for drags to go to the
cricket-ground; the wide-open windows with
their gay flowers, whence issue sounds and scents
of the heavy luncheons of the more languidly
inclined; the river swarming with boats of all
sorts and sizes; the Union rooms full of readers

leisurely scanning the papers or dipping into
the magazines, with ices or cigars to soothe or
sweeten the summer afternoons; the roads busy
with rattling pony-carriages bound for Wood-
stock or Abingdon, Witney or Thame; even the
shops themselves are full, whose windows from
without and wares within tempt the passing
" loafer." " Where are the reading men ?" the
stranger may well ask.

There are plenty of them if you know where
to find them. But it is just because the stranger
is a stranger that he won't find them. What
can he know of the hours of heavy work got
through in the quiet of those bright summer
afternoons; of the one close-shut room on this
deserted staircase of open, idle doors; of that
back-quad attic, with its sported oak; of the
" coach's " crowded chambers, where, unheeding
the charms of river or cricket-field, of Union-
garden or leafy roads, he and his hourly pupils
sit, " grinding for the schools "?

Besides, the surprised and maybe shocked
stranger must remember that a large number of
men who come to Oxford do not come there
merely for the sake of the degree. They take

one if they can; the sooner they can, so much
the better are they pleased. They come to be
made men and gentlemen. A degree is only
one of the many means to that end. It is only
because some make it their all-absorbing motive
that the University sends forth into the world
so many prigs.

Within the first week Frank had made many
friends, most of them friends of Crawford's, who
had called at his suggestion. The secretaries of
the Boat and Cricket Clubs had looked him up,
to whom Frank, with much pleasure, had paid
his entrance fee and annual subscriptions.

The captain of the Paul's company in the Rifle
Corps had come to work upon his military ardour;
the president of the College Debating Society,
to arouse his ambition for oratory; the collector
for the various Church Societies, to test his
impartiality and charity. Frank was enabled, by
his father's wish and the means he had placed
at his disposal, to join the various societies, and
pay the subscriptions. But it was not this
pecuniary willingness alone that gained for our
freshman so much popularity. The pecuniary
outlay was as follows :—

E

	£	s.	d.
Boat Club	3	10	0
Cricket Club . . ·.	2	10	0
Paul's Debating Society . .	0	2	6
Union Society	1	5	0
Rifle Corps, including Band-Subscriptions and Uniform .	5	0	0

There is no need to enter into Frank's charitable subscriptions. They were neither large nor small, but what they were, were given with pleasure. About this time also came in the valuation of his rooms, amounting to 30*l.* Our freshman is now, therefore, fairly started on his career.

CHAPTER IV.

THE EIGHTS.

April slipped away, and it was the evening of the 30th. Frank had dined in Hall; he had been to all his lectures that morning. He knew the work for the next day. There was no need, therefore, he thought, for further work. Turning out of the Lodge-gates, hardly knowing where he was going, he strolled into the High; and just by Spiers' he met a new acquaintance—Morton, of Magdalen.

"Where are you off, Ross?" he asked.

"Don't know," answered Frank; "nowhere particular."

The fact is, Frank had been drifting of late into these evening rambles to "nowhere particular." And a good deal of time they occupied too.

"You'd better come down to my rooms. I've got one or two fellows coming in for a hand at whist."

Frank, not being the impossible model young man of the story-books, did not resist the invitation, but, linking his arm into Morton's, went off to Magdalen. The April night was not so warm that a fire was not pleasant. Morton's rooms were in the old quad, looking out towards the new buildings and the deer-park. The curtains were drawn and the lights burning. Several little tables were laid with dessert, and one cleared in the centre of the room, with packs of cards upon it. There were about a dozen men present.

Dessert over, cards began; but it was not whist. Everybody voted that slow. Frank himself thought that he never had played so enticing a game as loo. When he knocked in that night at five minutes to twelve, he fancied the porter eyed him suspiciously and knew that he had returned *minus* a few pounds and *plus* a racking headache. His suspicions were right. Few read more rightly or more quickly the character and career of the undergraduates than the porters who open to them nightly.

But, in spite of his headache, Frank managed to be up at four o'clock next morning. He had accepted Morton's invitation to breakfast at six, after hearing the choir sing the May-Morning Hymn on the college tower. George, the porter, as he opened the Lodge-gates to Frank and others, thought, in spite of his pale face, that he at least could not have been up to much mischief last night, or he would not have been up so early after it. And George, usually infallible, began to retract his last night's opinion.

As he stood on the leads and looked down through the grey battlements on the faint fresh green that was brightening the trees in the Botanical Gardens; on the distant spires and towers; and on the less fortunate crowds in the street below; and as the sweet voices of the choir rose and blended through the soft morning air, a feeling, whether it was regret or remorse he hardly knew, came over him. Anyhow he felt that this was a sweeter, purer pleasure than the gambling of last night, and confessed to himself that he had been "an utter fool for his pains."

It was a blazing afternoon about the end of May. The river—meaning thereby the Isis, the main river, to distinguish it from its tributary the Cherwell—was deserted save for a few energetic men in outrigged skiffs practising for sculling races, and the boatmen, in charge of the various college barges, sweltering in the sun, and, as fast as the heat would allow them, making preparations for the work of the evening. The Cherwell, with its slow, shady stream, its winding banks and drooping trees, was the favourite resort, but even here all was quiet. Every now and then a canoe flashed by lazily, or a punt plunged up in search of some cool nook. There was a momentary disturbance, perhaps, as it bumped against one already moored; and pairs of sleepy eyes would look up to scowl at the new-comer, if a stranger; or greet him lazily if a friend.

Just in one of the pleasantest corners, Frank and Monkton had fixed their craft, and were lying face upwards on a couple of enormous cushions —Monkton smoking or pretending to smoke; Frank reading or pretending to read.

" Are you going to stay for the Eights ?" asked Monkton.

" Rather," answered Frank. " Why ? aren't you ?"

" No, not I ! In the first place, I don't care about them ; and in the second place, I've promised Morton to drive to Abingdon at seven. It'll be getting cool then."

"It seems to me you're rather fond of going to Abingdon," answered Frank. "What's the attraction ? "

"My dear boy, ask no questions and I'll tell you no lies "—and at that moment a punt ran right into them.

"Now then, sir, look ahead ! " spluttered Monkton as their punt was nearly upset, and his cigar falling from his mouth burnt a small hole in his flannel trousers. The intruder apologized and plunged on again to disturb the rest of other unlucky beings.

"Well," went on Frank, " I'm glad I've not to pay your bill for pony-traps, that's all."

"Oh, well, as far as that goes," retorted Monkton, waking up a little, "that don't trouble me. I patronize the trustful Traces, and I'm sure the trustful one would be quite embarrassed if I offered to pay him ; so I don't. That's all."

"Does your governor give you an allowance ? " asked Frank.

"Not he. He told me not to get into debt, and to send in the bills. And a fellow can't live like a hermit. I've always had a horse at home, so I don't see why I shouldn't have one here. But I'm not proud, and so I hire a pony instead, and I'm sure the old man ought not to mind."

"Come out of that, you lazy young beggar!" called a voice in Frank's ears, and looking up he saw Crawford in one of those little cockle-shells in which Mr. Verdant Green so highly distinguished himself—"Aren't you coming down to see the Eights?"

Monkton looked at Crawford with that expression of half insolence, half fear, which characterizes so many freshmen, and drawled out,—

"Yes; Ross is going. He's so energetic, you know."

"That's a blessing, at all events," answered Crawford, "as long as there are fellows like you, about."

"By Jove!" said Frank, pulling out his watch, "it's getting late. If you're going to Abingdon at seven, Monkton, you'll have to look sharp."

"Going to Abingdon?" asked Crawford, half to himself, and getting no answer from Monkton.

"Look here! I say, you fellows! can't you

manage to get this punt back to the barges, and let me cut up through the meadows?" said Monkton. "I promised to be in Morton's rooms at half-past six, and it's just on six now."

"All right," said Frank, "Crawford will help me back with the punt"—really glad to get rid of him, for his younger and his older friend did not hit it off exactly.

"It strikes me that young man is beginning rather early," said Crawford paternally, as he lashed his boat to the punt and got in, much to Frank's relief, for it was his first day in a punt.

The latter did not say much, for he had himself commenced various extensive dealings with the trustful tradesmen—trustful, that is, for two years, but most distrustful afterwards—and he feared questioning and an inevitable lecture from Crawford.

By the time they reached the barges, the river and banks were getting crowded. The band was assembling on the 'Varsity barge (that belonging to the University Boat Club); and all the other college barges were in a bustle of excitement. It was "the first night of the Eights," and many

were the attempts to explain that somewhat ellip-
tical phrase to the uninitiated matrons and
maidens who were flocking from every quarter of
the town.

Just at the mouth of the Cherwell, Crawford
and Frank met a party of ladies and escorted
them to the Paul's barge ; and the latter, though
he fancied he was clear as to the meaning of
" Eights " and " Torpids," was really not sorry
to overhear his friend's explanation.

" You see," Crawford was saying to a pretty
girl with bright blue eyes, that certainly did not
seem to be reminded that they could see—" You
see, every college, that is athletic enough, has a
Boat Club; the best eight oars, rowers I mean, con-
stitute ' *the* Eight ;' the second best eight are ' the
Torpid.' The Torpid-races, or as we call them,
' the Torpids,' take place in the Lent term ; every
college that has an Eight and a Torpid enters the
latter for the Torpid-races ; and then they all row
to see which is best. Then in the Summer term
' the Eights ' are on ; that is the races of the college Eight-oars ; to-night is the first night, you
know. All the Eights are going to row to see
which is best."

"Yes; but," said Blue-eyes, "why do they have more than one race?"

"Well, you see"—Crawford could not help the phrase—"that is—er—it's rather difficult to explain."

But after a moment he took courage, and plunged into his explanation, which was to this effect, and which may assist the uninitiated reader.

The river is too narrow to admit of boats racing abreast. They are therefore arranged one behind the other, there being 120 feet from the nose of one to the stern of the other. All start simultaneously, the object of each being to "bump"—i.e. run into and touch the one in front of it. When a "bump" has taken place, both the "bumper" and the "bumped" row to the bank to let the others pass. There is a post opposite the barges, where most of the spectators sit, and when once a boat has passed this it cannot be bumped. The following night—called "night," but really meaning seven o'clock—the boats all start, with this exception, that if, for example, on Monday Balliol has bumped Christ-Church, on Tuesday Balliol will start ahead of

Christ-Church. The latter then has the chance of regaining its position by bumping Balliol, but it is also exposed to the danger of being bumped by the next boat. This goes on, in the case of the " Torpid," for six days; of the " Eights," for eight " nights." At the end, the boat that finishes with all the others behind it, holds the proud position of " Head of the River " for the year. It may have gained this by making " bumps," or by avoiding being " bumped." How the order was, in the origin of the races, settled, it is impossible to say; but it is the rule that any college club which " puts on "—i.e. enters a boat for the races—for the first time shall start at the bottom. Perhaps, after this explanation, any remaining difficulty will be cleared up by suggesting, as an illustration, a school-class, in which a place is gained for a successful answer. The boats, by " bumping " and being " bumped," respectively gain and lose places.

Crawford was rowing in the Brasenose Eight. So, after seeing his lady friends to seats on the top of the college barge, he ran down-stairs to dress for the race. The men who rowed in the Brasenose Eight and Torpid were unlike the

majority of men of other colleges, in that they
walked to the river in *mufti*, and put on their
boating-clothes in their barge. Frank, pleading
an excuse that he wanted to go down the Berkshire bank to see the start, but chiefly because
he was rather shy, left Crawford's party to the
attention of some other men, and, crossing in old
George West's punt, was soon lost in the crowd.

One by one the boats paddled down to the
start, cheered by their own men as they passed.
The crowd thickened. A great surging mass
pressed up against the rails that enclosed the
barges, and gazed enviously at the lucky ones
within the enclosure. A black line went coiling
down the pathway towards Iffley. Those were
the men who would see the start, and run back
with the boats to cheer them on. Presently there
was a great silence. Everybody was looking
right away to the Iffley Willows, or at watches.
Then the first gun went. Conversation flowed
again for four minutes. Then the one-minute
gun—and then utter silence, till with the third
boom a roar of voices began, that came nearer
and louder as the great black line began coiling
home again, as fast as it could.

Brasenose was Head of the River; and Blue-eyes was wearing the Brasenose colours; and Blue-eyes' heart, though she would not have confessed it, was in a flutter of excitement. On came the boats. Balliol was close behind Brasenose. The Brasenose men on bank and barge shouted. The Balliol men shouted more loudly. They must catch them. Blue-eyes hated the Balliol men; but, for all that, the nose of the Balliol boat was within a foot of the Brasenose rudder. Now it overlapped it, but failed to touch it, for the Brasenose coxswain, by a sharp pull of the rudder-string, turned a rush of water against their nose and washed them off.

The Brasenose men yelled till Blue-eyes felt the drums of her little ears were nigh to cracking. And then Crawford, who was rowing stroke, seemed to pull himself together for a final effort, and laying himself well out, gave his men a longer stroke. Now they were clear—now there was a foot between them—now two—now three. Then he quickened: his men answered bravely. Foot by foot they drew ahead, and when they were on the post, Balliol was a good length behind. Blue-eyes had often heard, "See, the Conquering Hero comes," but she could not make out why the sound of it now gave her a choking feeling in the throat. Certainly she saw no more of the races, though boat by boat came by, each in as keen pursuit of the one just in advance of it as Balliol had been to catch Brasenose.

There was a merry party that night in Crawford's rooms, and Blue-eyes sat by the host, and was highly amused at the plain fare he was obliged to eat in the midst of the dainties of the supper-table; and she was half inclined to be cross when at a quarter to ten the captain of the Boat Club, who was present, firmly but politely suggested the breaking up of the party—"unless," he explained, "you want to see Brasenose go down to-morrow night."

But men must work, or at any rate go in for examinations, whatever the women may do. So the "Eights" passed away, and Blue-eyes returned to her home, taking with her, from many, the sunshine she had brought. The Proctor's notices recalled Frank and several hundred other unfortunates to the stern realities of University life. Parted for a while in the all-too-brief days of Blue-eyes' supremacy, Monkton and Frank drifted together again by the force of kindred obligations. Together they went to the Junior Proctor, and entered their names for Responsions (commonly called "Smalls," "because such a werry small number on 'em gets through," as the guides will tell you); together they parted with the statutable guinea, fondly hoping that in due time they would get a tangible result in the shape of a testamur. Together they gazed admiringly, nor yet without awe, at their names when they appeared in the Gazette; and together, in white ties and "garments of a subfusc hue," as prescribed by the statutes, they proceeded one bright morning in June to the Schools. There for two days, from nine to twelve, and from half-past one to half-past three, they were examined by papers. Then, after waiting a few days, Monkton's *vivâ voce* came on, the order of this being alphabetical. But when at two o'clock the same day the Clerk of the Schools read out a list of those who had passed, and for the gladly-paid shilling handed over a small piece of blue paper, testifying the fact in the handwriting of the much-enduring Examiners, Monkton's testamur was, alas! not forthcoming. Frank did not pass as easily as he might have passed. The last few weeks had taken the polish off his work. He got his testamur, it is true, but he was rather ashamed of feeling relieved, for he knew that he ought never to have had any fears of failing in such a school-boy examination.

He called on his tutor to consult him as to his future work. The First Public Examination (commonly called Moderations) is, like Responsions, obligatory on all; but here the student may offer either the minimum amount of work, called "a Pass," or go in for Honours either in Classics or Mathematics. The Honours Examination is to chiefly test style of translation from Latin and Greek authors into English, and *vice versâ*, together with grammatical and critical questions bearing on the contents, style, and literary history of the books offered. Papers are also set in the Elements of Comparative Philology; the History of the Greek Drama, with Aristotle's Poetics; and the Elements of Deductive Logic, with either selections from the Organon, or from Mill's "Inductive Logic." The four Gospels in Greek, together with questions on the subject-matter, are compulsory on all,—Passmen and

Classmen alike. After the examination is over, the examiners (in this instance called Moderators) distribute the names of those whom they judge to have shown sufficient merit into three classes, the names in each class being arranged alphabetically. If a candidate is not good enough to be placed in a class, but has yet shown as much knowledge as is required of the ordinary Passmen, he receives a testamur to that effect. This is called a "gulf." The subjects for Pass Moderations are Latin Prose (rather more difficult than for Responsions); the elements of Logic, or Arithmetic and Algebra to Quadratic Equations; unseen passages of Greek and Latin; and three authors, of whom one must be Greek, and one must be either an Orator, Philosopher, or Historian.

After a little questioning, Mr. Wood's advice to Frank was to go in for a Pass, and, that over, to read for Honours in one of the Final Schools, such as Modern History or Law. The advice was wise, for his classical reading was not very much advanced; and even if he could have got through the bare reading of the necessary text-books, he would not have acquired the style of translation and elegance in composition needed for the highest honours.

He chose Logic in preference to Mathematics, by Mr. Wood's advice; and for his authors, Herodotus (Books V. and VI.); Livy (Books V., VI., and VII.), and Juvenal, certain Satires being omitted. Having purchased these books, and laid in a good store of industrious intentions, he left Oxford and his freshman's term behind him, not at all sorry to be going home.

CHAPTER V.

THE LONG VACATION.

THERE was a good deal of the schoolboy's pleasure in the commencement of the holidays, mixed with the pride that he felt in his new condition. There were only a few passengers for Porchester, and only a few people on the platform when he alighted; but the few there were knew him, and Oxford made the chief matter of their inquiries, and a pleasant topic for him to dilate upon. But he was soon hurried off by two of his admiring younger brothers, and seated at the side of old John, the factotum, in the pony-carriage, talking hard, now to him, now to his brothers, who sat behind. How familiar the road was! Did green hedges ever look so green as those? or was summer twilight ever so sweet as this that lay so peacefully about little Porchester? The old church-tower rose like a soft shadow from the close trees. There, beside it, peeped the vicarage gables and chimneys. There was old Sally, the laundress, resting at her gateway, rubbing her wrinkled fingers as though she would smooth away the signs of so much soap and water. There was the postmaster putting up the shutters of his little grocery-shop; the tailor in his garden, tending his standard roses; the blacksmith at his silent smithy; there were the carrier's horses just being unharnessed from the van that in these primitive parts was no mean rival of the railway. A few children here; a knot of women there, chattering, scolding, laughing, staring, questioning; there a group of men outside the "Anchor;" here some boys playing marbles.

How unchanged it all was! The term at Oxford seemed like a dream. Frank could scarcely believe he had been away more than two months.

Now they are passing the vicarage garden. The gate is open, and Frank, much to the amusement of Tom and Will in the hind-seat of the pony-carriage, stares hard through the white posts and up the lawn. Whatever his thoughts or hopes may have been, they are rudely interrupted (and most probably shattered) by a couple of voices from behind, which seem to be bubbling over with amusement, and to be jostling each other for the first and loudest place.

" She's away ! "

" Who's away ? " asked Frank quietly, with assumed indifference.

" Who's away ? " repeat the two behind. " Why, who're you looking for, eh ? "

" *Are* the vicarage people away, then ? " said Frank.

" Rose is," again comes from the bubbling voices.

But before the subject can be pursued further, old John, pointing with his whip, says,—

" There's the master, sir."

And Frank, looking straight away up the road, discerns his father coming towards them, and jumps out of the carriage.

" Why, Frank, my boy, I declare you've grown ! "

Nor did his dignity decline the honour. He took his father's arm, and, letting the younger ones drive home with John and the luggage, walked and talked with his father till they reached the house. His mother and sisters were at the door to welcome him. Never had there been such a pleasant, proud home-coming yet. The servants peeped from the upper windows to see "Master Frank," whom they doubtless expected to find completely transformed, and John, taking the luggage from the carriage, again took stock of him, and told the servants with an air that, as always, carried weight,—

"Arter all, there's no place like college to make a man of a young gentleman."

One scene more to complete the first act of our freshman's life.

Mr. Ross was, as became a lawyer, a man of sound business-like habits. Directly after breakfast on the following morning he called Frank into his study, and they went together through all the bills.

The result of their investigation was as follows :—

Travelling and Hotel Expenses at	£	s.	d.
Matriculation	5	10	0
Caution Money (to Paul's) . . .	30	0	0
Matriculation Fee (to the University) .	2	10	0
Glass and China (to the scout) . .	9	19	6

Cap and Gown	.	.	.	.	£1	2	6
Entrance Fee (Union Society)		.	.	1	5	0
Boat Club Subscription		.	.	3	10	0
Cricket Club	.	.	.	.	2	10	0
Paul's Debating Society		.	.	0	2	6
Rifle Corps .	.	.	.	.	5	0	0
Valuation of Furniture		.	.	30	0	0
Battels for Summer Term		.	.	35	0	0
Fee for Responsions	.	.	.	1	0	0
Books, Sundries, and Travelling Expenses .	.	.	.	.	10	0	0

The summer passed. Frank had been to the Henley Regatta at Crawford's invitation, and had stayed with him at the old "Red Lion" with various crews; had run down the bank at his side when he was practising for the Diamond Sculls in the sweet June mornings, and had shouted with the shouting crowd when he won the race, beating the London man and the Cantab who had been training "dark." Then he had gone to Crawford's home for a pleasant week; then back to little Porchester, where, with garden-parties and cricket, with boating on the river that seemed so deserted after the crowded Isis, and lawn-tennis, the time had passed away happily enough. Of work for the " Schools " Frank had done little or nought; but when in August the vicar's daughter left Porchester for six weeks, work somehow seemed easier, and he managed to get through a fair amount; and again, when the boys went back to school about the middle of September, and he was left alone with his parents and sisters, there seemed fresh opportunities for study. But then—but then back came the vicar's daughter, and books were again forgotten. The village seemed to have gained fresh beauties. Every old gate and stile seemed no longer made of common wood, every hedge no longer clad with common green. The organ-loft where she practised in the week was no longer a dusty, dark, break-neck place, but the place for breaking something which, whatever lovers may say, is often easily mended by

"Time and the change the old man brings."

And what a poet Frank was in those days! How he idealized, and in his own fashion glorified, every little winding woodland path, every glimpse of wold seen through the fading autumn leaves, every stretch of quiet river, the old boats, the crumbling bridge, the dark weir, the church-tower—that useful part of a young poet's stock-in-trade.

In fact, when he returned to Oxford one Friday evening in October, he quite agreed with the old woman's and the sailor's superstition that Friday was an unlucky day; he wrapped himself in his rug, and felt that if his heart was not breaking, he was at least deeply in love. Silence was his consolation. He rejected the invitation of a friend whom he met *en route* to transfer himself and his goods to the atmosphere of a smoking compartment. He stared gloomily at the persistent bookstall-boys; rejected even the offer of a Banbury cake at Didcot. In his condition, there was something positively comforting in that most cheerless and wretched of all stations. The wind that moaned in the telegraph-wires seemed to murmur " Rose." The bell that rang violently in the platform-porter's hand seemed like the little single bell in Porchester Church—of course much louder and harsher to Frank's imagination, but it was a bell, and it recalled Rose, and that was enough.

Having passed safely through the turmoil of the Oxford platform, and the loneliness of Friday night, on Saturday morning he rushed precipitously to Davis's picture-shop in " the

Turl," [1] and having purchased a photograph of the Huguenot picture by Millais, hung it in a corner by his chimney looking-glass. In that corner his friends noticed he now was constantly to be found sitting. They, of course, did not know that in that picture Frank saw Rose and himself under the vicarage wall. He was at a loss, it is true, to account even to himself for the pocket-handkerchief which is being bound round the reluctant arm. But what mattered to him such a paltry detail, even though it made the whole gist of the picture?

Term began with the usual routine. Chapel at half-past eight on Saturday evening, at which all assembled except a few who were detained by those convenient "tidal trains," which always seem to be late when one is coming back from a Long-Vacation scamper on the Continent, or from the injured Emerald Isle, but never when one is thither bound.

And then comes Sunday morning, with the many good-intentioned ones hurrying to their seats past the much-enduring Bible-clerk, whose

[1] Turl Street. High Street is "the High;" Broad Street, "the Broad," in Oxford vernacular.

labours would, however, very soon lessen with the growth of term;—Sunday, with the heavy luncheon;—Sunday, with the long constitutional in the bright October sunlight—was a first Sunday in Michaelmas Term ever other than a bright one? Dinner in Hall at six, with the endless greetings that the confusion of Chapel had prevented. Monday morning, with its formal calls on Master and Dean, Tutor and Lecturer; and Monday evening, with its posted list of lectures, club-meetings, and subscriptions; till Tuesday morning comes, with the greater or less obedience of the victims of those various calls, shows that term has begun in very earnest, no matter whether the earnestness be the earnestness of industry or of that which flourishes as abundantly —idleness.

CHAPTER VI.

"THE FLYING TERMS."

It was a Thursday night; and the rooms of the "Union" were crowded, for the debate was to be opened by a popular member. A few men were in the reading-rooms, indifferent to the subject and its mover; a few were in the writing-room, hurrying over their letters, in order to be in time for the "private business," which is usually the most amusing part of the evening's proceedings. There were several important telegrams posted in the Hall, and the stopping of members to read them considerably added to the general confusion. Ladies were hurrying upstairs to the little uncomfortable gallery,[1] with amused looks of curiosity, or the calm equanimity of accustomed visitors.

[1] The new Debating Hall, now (October) almost complete, will provide ample accommodation for visitors.

No one to-night waited to read, either for edification or for amusement, the endless notices of those private tutors, to whom advertisement seems a dire necessity—those manifestos of all shades, pleading, peremptory, apologetic, confidential, and confident, which suggest the question :—" Where are the pupils, to be instructed by these willing and anxious instructors ? "

The steward's room is in possession of two attendants only, for the steward and his indefatigable son are upstairs in the committee-room, in attendance upon the committee.

It is eight o'clock, and the debating-room is crammed. Every seat is filled ; but those for whom there are not seats are quite content to stand. The gallery is fringed with women's faces, looking down upon the mass of men below. There is a murmur of suppressed conversation, which suddenly ceases on the cry of " Order." The president enters, followed by the treasurer, librarian, and most of the members of the committee. He is in evening dress—the exception and not the rule; in his case it is the sign of honour. He has been dining, for the first time, at the High table of the college which has just elected

him Fellow. To-night is his first public appearance since his election, and, being a popular man
and officer, he is loudly cheered. The officers
seat themselves, and in a moment the president
rises and proclaims " Order," and the business of
the evening commences. He first reads a list of
those members of the University proposed for
election, and those already elected, and then calls
upon the librarian to bring forth his list of books.
That officer, a big-headed, ungainly man, with a
squint, hurries through a list, to which prices and
particulars are appended, and then asks any, who
wish, to challenge any book or books. If any are
challenged, they are temporarily withdrawn from
the list, and the rest are put to the vote and
carried ; after which the objections are made to
the particular books before challenged, and are
met by the librarian with considerable ability, and
the books, with one exception, carried. He then
rises to propose " That ' The Gorgon Head ' (much
laughter), by Mr. Tennyson Jones, presented by
the author to the library, be accepted by the
society, and that a vote of thanks be given to the
honourable member for his present."

No one wishing to challenge this proposition,

it is formally put and carried, with faint cheering.

The president then rises: " Does any honourable member wish to put any question to the officers of this society relative to their official duties ? "

At least a dozen members rise in different parts of the room—we beg pardon—the House.

A red-headed young gentleman, with spectacles, catches first the president's eye, and is put in possession of the House. His voice is high and shrill.

" Sir—"

" Hear! hear! " from several facetious members encouragingly.

" Sir—I wish to ask the honourable treasurer —(loud cries of ' Speak up, sir ')—I wish to ask the honourable treasurer—"

" Hear ! hear ! " from a stentorian voice in one corner.

" Order ! order ! "

" Sir," again resumes the luckles red-headed inquirer, " I—I—have lost my umbrella. I—I— put it in the stand on Wednesday evening— ('Hear! hear!')—on my way to—to—the smoking-room, and—and—and—it was not there when I came back." And the speaker drops into his seat.

The treasurer takes no notice, but the president rises and says:—"I must remind the honourable member that any statement he may have to make must be introduced or followed by a question."

The owner of the lost umbrella rises, and before he has opened his mouth is told to "speak up." This time he does speak up, in very shrillness: "I wish to ask the honourable treasurer whether he will take some steps for the recovery of my umbrella."

The treasurer is a stout youth, short of speech and of stature. He clips his sentences: "I must remind the honourable member that this society is not a police institution. I regret the loss of his umbrella. I regret still more that there are members in this society so careless or so dishonest as to remove umbrellas not belonging to them."

"Sir"—from another corner—"I consider the answer of the honourable treasurer most unsatisfactory. I now beg to ask him whether he will

G

take steps to prevent the robbery—('Oh! oh!')
—yes—robbery of the property of members of
this society."

The treasurer is again on his legs: "In answer
to the last honourable member, I beg to say that
as far as I know anything of the funds of this
society, it is not in a position to pay for police-
men to guard the umbrellas of honourable
members. If honourable members value their
umbrellas, I should recommend them to leave
them in the steward's room, or carry them with
them into whichever of the society's rooms they
may go."

"Sir"—from another quarter—"will you move
for a committee of inquiry into the loss of
umbrellas and other property?" (Loud cheers.)

By this time the treasurer is white-hot:—"No,
sir!" and he flumps into his chair—(loud cheers
from the treasurer's partisans and from the
admirers of his doggedness). He is not, however,
yet done with.

"I beg to ask the honourable treasurer,"
says a grimy-looking youth, "why there are so
few nail-brushes in the lavatory?" (Roars of
laughter.)

"In answer to the honourable member," says the treasurer, "I beg to state that I have already given orders for a fresh and—as they seem so much in request—a still larger supply." (Cheers.)

Then there is a brief space of silence.

"Does any other honourable member wish to put any questions to the officers of this society relative to their official duties?"

No one rising, the president says—

"The House will now proceed to public business;" and after waiting a few seconds, to give those who wish the chance to leave, he reads from a notice-board,—

"The motion before the House is, 'That the present Ministry is unworthy of the confidence of this House and of the nation,' moved by Mr Dubber, of Trinity."

There is a perfect uproar as Mr. Dubber rises and moves towards the table—cheers from his supporters, groans from his opponents; but he is too accustomed to the temper of his audience to take any notice. He pours out a glass of water and leisurely drinks half the contents, and waits confidently. His confidence commands atten-

tion; and in a clear, ringing voice, he proceeds to
rattle away a clever *résumé* of the stump speeches
of his political party. There is no lack to-night
of speakers. No less than six rise directly he sits
down.

And so the debate goes on unflaggingly until
half-past ten, when, there being no more speakers,
the mover replies; and then the president reads
the motion once more, and says,—

"Those who are in favour of this motion will
say 'Aye;' those who are against it will say
'No.'"

There are nearly 500 members present, and the
noise may be imagined.

"The 'Noes' have it," is the president's
ruling.

"Divide! divide!" from the "Ayes;" and the
president accordingly gives the order,—

"Those who are in favour of this motion will
go to the right of the chair; those who are against
it to the left."

Then follows a scene of indescribable confusion. In about ten minutes' time the numerous
tellers have agreed, and the president reads the
numbers,—

"Those who are in favour of this motion, 179; those who are against it, 290. The motion is therefore lost."

Loud cheers, and the House separates.

Within a few days of the commencement of term, Frank had found his name posted for rowing—that is, for rowing under the direction of the senior men who were coaching the likely freshmen for the Torpid races, which would come off in the ensuing Lent Term; and he took so kindly to the work that he was soon regularly among the recognized set from which the crew would eventually be picked. In fact, his performances had attracted the notice of the president of the University Boat Club, and he had been "down" with the men who were being coached with a view to rowing against Cambridge. This was indeed an honour; and he strained every energy to get chosen for one of the Trial Eights that were to race at the end of term, and from which the University Eight (commonly called "the 'Varsity") would be selected.

His wishes were fulfilled, and he was put No. 6 in what was supposed to be the better of the two boats. This, of course, insured his rowing in his College Torpid next term, and in his College Eight in the summer term, and it might have led to a seat in "the 'Varsity."

As a matter of fact, it did not; but Frank was well content with the honour of merely rowing in the "Trials," and more especially as the Eight in which he was rowing won the race in November. Towards the close of term he was made a Free-mason, and very proud he was to tell his father, himself a Mason of some distinction, the various gossip of his lodge, "The Apollo," which claims among its members some of England's best-known brethren.

One other little distinction Frank had to relate on going down for the Christmas vacation, and that was the flattering notice, in the *Under-graduate's Journal*, of a poem of his which had appeared in the University magazine, *College Rhymes;* [1] and it may safely be asserted that no one in Porchester was prouder of the poet than the vicar's daughter, who saw herself reflected in the mirror of his verse.

The Christmas vacation passed. Lent Term came, and with it the Torpids. Paul's made five

[1] Now—*O tempora ! O mores !*—defunct.

bumps, and Frank duly posted copies of the *Undergraduate's Journal*, which recorded the fact, to the vicarage and to his home. But with this proud event he abandoned for the present most of his amusements, confined himself to the practice for the Eights which were coming off in May, and to his work for Moderations, which was fixed for about the same date. The college lectures not being sufficient, he found himself obliged to "put on a coach"—i. e. employ a private tutor—during the summer term; but when he got his "testamur" in June, just a week before Commemoration, he and his father both felt that the ten guineas [1] had been profitably expended.

[1] The customary fee for a term's private tuition, consisting of three lessons weekly, of one hour each.

CHAPTER VII.

A READING PARTY.

MODERATIONS being thus thrown behind, the next step was the choice of subjects in which to take a degree. For the Second Public or Final Examination for the degree of B.A. there is yet further scope of subject allowed. Here, again, a student has the option of taking a Pass or an Honour Degree; and here also both Passmen and Classmen alike have to pass an examination in the Rudiments of Faith and Religion, the subjects of which are :—

(1) The Books of the Old and New Testament.
(2) The Holy Gospels and Acts of the Apostles in the original Greek.
(3) The Thirty-nine Articles.

But any candidate may for himself, or his parents or guardians for him, object on religious grounds

to this examination, and in this case he is allowed
to offer some books or subjects appointed for
this purpose by the Board of Studies.

The subjects for the Pass Degree are arranged
in three groups, as follows, the books specified
being those which may now be offered till further
notice :—

GROUP A.

(1) Two books, either both Greek, or one Greek and one
Latin ; one being a Greek philosophical work, and the
other a Greek or Latin historian.

> *e.g.* Aristotle's Ethics, Books i.—iv., together with
> chapters 6—10 of Book x.
> Aristotle's Politics, Books i., iii., vii.
> Plato—Republic, Books i.—iv.
> Herodotus—Books vii.—ix.
> Livy, Books xxi.—xxiv.
> Tacitus—Annals, Books i.—iv.

With questions on the subject-matter of the books
offered.

(2) The outlines of Greek and Roman History, with a special
period of one or the other, and English Composition.

> *e.g.* Greek—from the Legislation of Solon to the
> death of Alexander the Great.
> Roman—from the establishment of the Republic
> to the death of Domitian.

Special periods.

> Greek—the Persian war; the Peloponnesian war.
> Roman—the second Punic war; the reign of
> Tiberius.

Group B.

(1) Either English History and a period or subject of English Literature, or a period of modern European History, with Political and Descriptive Geography, with English Composition in each case.

> *e.g.* English History to 1815, with one of the following :—
>
> > (*a*) Piers Ploughman—the Prologue, Passus i.—vii.; Chaucer—the Prologue, the Knightes Tale, the Nonne Prestes Tale.
> >
> > (*b*) Shakespeare—The Tempest, King Lear, Richard II., Hamlet.
> >
> > (*c*) Dryden — Selections ; Pope — Essay on Man, Epistles and Satires.

(2) French or German, including Composition and a period of Literature.

> *e g.* Molière, Le Tartuffe; Corneille, Les Horaces, *or* Racine, Athalie ; Voltaire, Siècle de Louis XIV., Chapters i.—xxiv., with a general acquaintance with the History and Literature of the Age of Louis XIV.; unseen passages of French : *or*, Schiller, the Maid of Orleans ; Goethe, Hermann and Dorothea, *or* Lessing, Nathan der Weise ; Goethe, Wahrheit und Dichtung, Books i.—iv., with a general acquaintance with the History of the Classical period of German Literature (from Klopstock to Goethe); unseen passages of German.

(3) The Elements of Political Economy, to be read in Faw-

cett's Manual, and Adam Smith's "Wealth of Nations,"
Books i. and ii.

(4) Either Stephen's "Blackstone," Book ii., *or* Justinian's
"Institutes," omitting from Book ii., tit. 11, to Book
iii., tit. 12.

GROUP C.

(1) The Elements of Geometry, including Geometrical
Trigonometry.

(2) The Elements of Mechanics, solid and fluid, treated
mathematically.

(3) The Elements of Chemistry, with a practical examination.

(4) The Elements of Physics, not necessarily treated mathematically.

Of the above subjects in the three groups each
candidate is examined in three, of which not more
than two can be taken from any one of the three
groups, and of which one must be either A (1) or
B (2). The examinations in the three subjects
may be passed in separate terms.

The commonest selections made are as follows :—

GROUP A (1).
GROUP B (3) and (4).

Those men who prefer History will naturally
offer the outlines of Ancient History, as it works
well with the text-books in Group A (1). Those

who are going to the Bar or to be admitted as solicitors will naturally offer one of the branches of Law, the Roman Law being especially the favourite with Bar-students, as the Roman Law Bar Examination may be studied for and passed almost simultaneously. The choice for the Classman lies among the following :—

1. LITERÆ HUMANIORES, including—
    (1) The Greek and Latin Languages.
        (*a*) Specified books and books not specially offered.
        (*b*) Translations into Greek and Latin Prose.
    (2) The Histories of Ancient Greece and Rome.
        (*a*) Specified periods.
        (*b*) General knowledge of Classical Geography and Antiquities.
    (3) Philosophy.
        (*a*) Logic.
        (*b*) The outlines of Moral Philosophy.
        (*c*) The outlines of Political Philosophy.

3. MATHEMATICS.
        (*a*) Elementary Pure Mathematics.
        (*b*) Elementary Mechanics of Solid and Fluid Bodies.
        (*c*) Pure Mathematics.
        (*d*) Mechanics of Solid and Fluid Bodies.
        (*e*) Optics, Geometrical and Physical.
        (*f*) Newton's Principia and Astronomy.

4. NATURAL SCIENCE.

> Preliminary : Mechanics.
> Physics.
> Chemistry.
> Final : Physics.
> Chemistry.
> Biology.

And the following special subjects :—

> (*a*) Crystallography and Mineralogy.
> (*b*) Geology and Palæontology.
> (*c*) Zoology.
> (*d*) Botany.

—taken respectively as supplementary to the general subjects.

5. JURISPRUDENCE.

> (1) General Jurisprudence.
>> The principles of Jurisprudence, the theory of Legislation, and the early history of Legal Institutions. Special reference to Austin's Lectures, Bentham's Principles of Morals and Legislation, and the works of Sir Henry Maine.

> (2) History of English Law.
>> (*a*) Constitutional Law.
>>> The leading principles and the following topics :—Legislative power of Parliament, the modes in which it is exercised, and its extent as to territory and persons.
>>> The prerogatives of the Crown, the privileges of the Houses of Parliament.

The constitutional position of the Privy
Council, the Ministers of the Crown,
the Established Church, the Courts of
Law, and the Armed Forces.

Reference to Blackstone or Stephens'
"Commentaries," Stubbs' "Documents
Illustrative of English History," Hal-
lam's "Constitutional History," and Sir
.T. E. May's "Constitutional History."

The following statutes must be carefully
read: Constitutions of Clarendon. Magna
Charta, Stat. Westminster II. 13 Ed. 1,
Stat. 1, c. 24. Petition of Right. Habeas
Corpus Act, 31 Car. II. c. 2. Bill of
Rights, 1 W. and M. Sess. 2, 2. Act of
Settlement, 12 and 13 Will. III. c. 2.

b) History of the Law of Real Property.

Reference to Blackstone or Stephens'
"Commentaries," Digby's "Introduction to the History of Real Property."
Principal statutes referred to in the latter must be mastered, and reference may
with advantage be made to Williams'
"Treatise on the Law of Real Property."

.(3) Roman Law.

The Institutes of Gaius.

The Institutes of Justinian.

(4) English Law.

The principles of the Law of Contracts.

(5) International Law.

(*a*) The outlines of International Law as a
system.

 (*b*) The history of the law relating to seas, ships,
   and navigable rivers in time of peace:
   Reference to Woolsey's "Introduction," and
   Heffter's "Europäisches Völkerrecht,"
   Wheaton's "Elements," or "Law of Nations," by Sir Travers Twiss. On subject
   (*b*) "Ortolan's "Diplomatie de la Mer,"
   livre deuxième.

6. MODERN HISTORY.
 (1) The continuous History of England.
 (2) General History during some selected period.
 (3) A special portion of History or a special Historical
   subject, carefully studied with reference to
   original authorities.
 (4) Political Economy, Constitutional Law, and Political and Descriptive Geography.
 (5) A subject or period of Literature (optional).

7. THEOLOGY.
 (1) The Holy Scriptures (the New Testament in the
   Greek).
 (2) Dogmatic and Symbolic Theology.
 (3) Ecclesiastical History and the Fathers.
 (4) The Evidences of Religion.
 (5) Liturgies.
 (6) Sacred Criticism and the Archæology of the Old
   and New Testaments.

 Knowledge of Hebrew has great weight in the distribution
of Honours.

Frank had always intended to go in for one of
the Honour Schools, but agreed with his father

that there was no necessity to avail himself of the longest allowance of time granted. He need not present himself for three years, but his father decided that two years was quite long enough, in addition to the year he had already spent. He must do what he could in the two years.

There was no dispute between father and son. Their views corresponded. Frank was to be called to the Bar, and the Honour School of Law was chosen for the degree. The subjects for this would, in a great measure, answer the further purpose of the Bar Call Examination. Mr. Ross proposed to enter Frank's name at the Inner Temple in the ensuing Michaelmas Term. He should then " eat dinners " during the two years in which he was reading for his Oxford degree; that taken, he should have one year's reading in a barrister's chambers. This, he considered, ought to qualify him not only in book-work, but practically for a call. Moreover, it would give him just the necessary time to complete the statutable number of terms.

Frank was anxious to enter at once, before the Trinity Term was over, but on this point his father was firm. There was no need for such immediate hurry. As it was, he would be qualified for a call, at an age considerably below the average. Mr. Ross had noticed that the first Long Vacation had been, comparatively speaking, wasted. He had said nothing, but had resolved that the second and third should not be a repetition of the first. He therefore directed Frank to write to his college tutor, Mr. Woods, for particulars of the subjects for the Honour Law School, and for advice as to a "coach" for part of the Long Vacation; and he himself wrote to his old friend, Mr. Wodehouse, on the latter point.

Frank's letter from Mr. Woods was as follows :—

" Paul's.

" DEAR MR. ROSS,—I am very glad to hear that you have so soon made up your mind as to the subjects in which you propose to take your degree; and I have no doubt your father's plan of entering you at the Inner Temple next Michaelmas Term is a wise one.

" Mr. Edwards, of University College, is, I have every reason to believe, a most advisable Law ' coach.' He is just now arranging a reading party to Switzerland, and I should hope your father will consent to your joining. Tell him from me that reading parties are not what they were in my undergraduate days—mere pleasure-trips, in which work forms the very last consideration. The few men now who

II

go with a reading party really go to read. You may mention my name in writing to Mr. Edwards. He will, of course, furnish you with all particulars.

> "Believe me, yours sincerely,
>
> · "J. Woods."

The letter from Mr. Wodehouse was characteristic :—

> "Dear Mr. Ross,—Law is not my line, or I would take your boy myself; but I know an excellent coach, Edwards of University, who is now settling a reading party, for Switzerland, I believe. Send your boy with him ; you can't do better. I send by this post a copy of the Examination Regulations, revised to this date. Details, of course, you will get from Edwards.
>
> "I am yours truly,
>
> "Philip Wodehouse."

After the letters, there was not much difficulty in deciding that Edwards was the coach to be secured. But the Swiss tour ! Frank said nothing, nor did Mr. Ross—the former because he knew his father's disposition, the latter because he would not promise what he might not be able, with justice to the rest of his family, to afford.

However, after a suspense of three days, Frank was summoned after breakfast to the study. His father had received a letter from the coach, telling him the probable cost of the tour, and he had decided to send Frank. The party would leave London on the 1st of July. They were to meet for dinner at the Grosvenor Hotel at six o'clock, and go from Victoria by the mail that catches the night-boat from Dover to Calais. Mr. Edwards added a few particulars as to books, and, rightly conjecturing this to be Frank's first journey abroad, some suggestions as to clothes and necessaries generally.

Mr. Ross winced a little when he heard the route that was chosen. But when he had made up his mind to an expense, he was not a man to worry over the inevitable extras.

The few days of June that remained passed quickly enough. Frank, somehow, was not at home as much as his brothers and sisters could have wished. At meals there were sundry questions as to his doings, amused looks at his evident confusion, till even Mr. Ross, usually oblivious to the jokes that passed between the young folks, questioned his wife as to their meaning.

When he heard the suggestion, he at first laughed at it as ridiculous, then said the whole affair was "out of the question," not from any dislike to Rose, for he was indeed very fond of her, and finally saying he would speak to Frank, said nothing after all.

*   *   *   *   *

It was a soft, sweet evening, that of June 30th, and Frank, having finished his packing, slipped out unnoticed after dinner. It was a difficult matter to avoid the prying eyes of his brothers, but the dessert that evening was unusually absorbing, and long after Mr. and Mrs. Ross had left the table, the boys were diligently making themselves ill. Seizing the opportunity, he was three fields beyond the paddock before his absence was even mentioned.

He was sad, down-hearted, romantically melancholy. And yet he had a delightful tour through Switzerland in store. Porchester had never seemed such a lovely little place. No Swiss mountains could ever have such beauty as those soft hills yonder; no glaciers the charm of the gently flowing river; no Alpine forests the sweetness of these English meadows, now silvering with the evening dew, and softening in the falling mist. He stopped by a gate. He found his initials cut there, just in one corner out of sight;

and near them one other letter. Three years ago
he had broken his best knife, and cut his finger,
over that little work. And there it was still—
lichened over now, but still legible. He would
not touch it. He wondered if it would still be
there when he came back. When he came back
Was the boy going to India for twenty years, or
to the North Pole? Who would touch the letters? Who would even read them? Who that
came by this way would be likely to stop by that
uninteresting gate, and draw aside those great
dock-leaves merely to see F. R. and R. clumsily
carved? And who, if they saw them, would
trouble to deface them?

But Frank was in love and was proportionately
melancholy. And lo! as in answer to his
thoughts, softly over the new-cut grass comes the
vicar's daughter.

It should be clearly understood that the pathway along which Rose came so opportunely was
public, though seldom frequented. It led from
the village of Porchester to a ferry, and this carried
you to a hamlet, Wood Green, that lay within
the vicar's ministrations. Just now there was
illness in the hamlet, and Rose used daily to visit

the sick. Frank, on no such journeys bent, passed many hours of those last days of June about the fields, and crossing and re-crossing in the ferry-boat. Luckily this was worked by a marvellous contrivance of wheels, ropes, and poles, and there was no observant Charon to wonder at, and then report, the strange and repeated passages of the lawyer's son. Last evening, at the same time and place, he had met Rose: had told her he was leaving for Switzerland: had gone so far as to ask her if she was going to Wood Green the next evening; and she, because she was Rose, told him yes. Perhaps there was another reason, the cause of which lay in him. But she never speculated. He had asked her, and she had told him. She was going to Wood Green, and why not say so?

They walked slowly, oh! so slowly, across the misty meadows. They crossed, as lazily as the stream would suffer them, the little ferry. They reached Wood Green. It was only a basket and a message that Rose had to deliver to-night, and Frank had not long to wait at the little white wicket at Vowles's cottage. Then back again, across the ferry, and up the fields; and then, just by the gateway where they had met, they stopped, and he showed her something, pulling aside the gigantic dock-leaves—three letters, rudely cut, and covered with lichen.

"I cut them three years ago," he said. "Was it very silly?"

"I don't know," she answered.

"I loved you then, Rose," he said softly, taking her hand, "but I love you a thousand times more now, darling."

And Rose has told him something that makes him utterly happy—something they have known these many weeks, but neither has dared to express. They are but children, but why should they not be happy? Only boy and girl, but is that any reason why their love should not be true? And so they walk back through the deepening summer night, he as proud as knight of old, and she as happy as any "fair ladye." And then by the vicarage garden-gate they say good-bye. They have not thought of the future. The present is theirs, and that is enough. She is a simple little village girl, and he an undergraduate; that is all. But "all" is a great deal to them.

At six o'clock in the evening of July 1st,

Edwards and his six pupils dined at the Grosvenor, wisely and not too well, in view of the passage that night. The party consisted of Hoskins of Brasenose, reading for Honours in Law; Lang and Kingdon of Christ Church, Maude of John's, and Royds of Exeter, reading for the Final Pass Schools; and Frank, who had thus one companion only in work. Edwards was quite a young man. He had been married about two years, but left his wife and child at home. He was just of an age not to be "donnish," and yet old enough to command a certain amount of necessary respect.

The pecuniary arrangements were as usual. Each was to pay his own personal expenses, and tuition-fee to Edwards at the rate of 10*l.* per month. But for the sake of convenience he would make the actual payments, and divide the amounts weekly.

At Victoria they broke up, for most of the men wanted to smoke. Edwards was not a smoker, and would have travelled to Dover alone had not Frank got into his compartment. The coach's weakness in this respect was the one little difficulty on the tour, and afforded a fund of amusement to the rest, who were young enough to re-

gard a non-smoker with feelings of surprise.
With the exception of Royds, none of the seven
had ever been abroad. He spoke French slightly,
and had a smattering of German. Edwards
could not speak a word of the former, but knew
enough of the latter for comfort in travelling.
No one else spoke either. Royds plumed himself
on his position of superiority, not without offence
to the rest of the party, who one and all joined in
snubbing him whenever he forgot his relation to
Edwards. He was just a source of a little
"pleasant acidity."

"I should advise you to lie down, if you're inclined to be sea-sick," said Royds, for the benefit
of the party generally, when they were on board.
"I never am."

Edwards retired to the centre of the boat;
Frank rolled himself in a rug on a bench near the
central deck cabins. The rest again consoled
themselves with cigars. The passage was long,
for the night was foggy; but the water was calm
as a duck-pond. Nevertheless, Royds looked
very pale as he landed at Calais.

They reached Paris in the early sweetness of
the morning. And what a charm the great city

has at that hour, and to first-comers! The brightness, the laughter, the sunshine of the town in its life! What a contrast to the death and dirt of London at such an hour!

They rushed across to an hotel near the Lyons Station, and after a hasty breakfast, breaking into three parties, drove all over the place, seeing, not " doing," as much as time allowed. In the evening they left for Geneva. Here they stayed two nights, and then went on to Chamounix by *diligence.* From Chamounix they ascended the Montanvert to cross the Mer de Glace.

This was their first climb. Royds, of course, had been before ; and with quite a paternal air he selected a guide one evening, and marshalled the party the following morning. Going up the pine-woods, their weary eyes were refreshed by the sight of three female figures. Without confessing as much to one another, they one and all quickened. But still those much-wished-for forms retreated, nor did they stop till the little hut on the top was reached. And then !—But we draw a veil. They were charming ladies, and delighted to see these gay young Englishmen. But, dear ladies ! they were not young. However, they were very pleasant, and the sound of the English tongue has a marvellous charm among foreigners.

The following morning, at ten o'clock, the corner by the Hôtel de l'Union was the centre of interest for the good folks of Chamounix. There at the hotel door stood seven sturdy mules and two guides. And presently, to the infinite delight of the bystanders, seven young Englishmen, followed by many packages, emerged and mounted. They were bound for Martigny, over the Col de Balme.

Poor guides! Unaccustomed to such riders, they started on their journey in happy ignorance. That evening, at seven o'clock, after a game struggle to keep within sight of their charges, they gave it up. And the cavalcade, headed by Edwards, putting their mules to their utmost speed (no contemptible pace considering their day's work), raced wildly by the wondering villagers into Martigny. Knapsacks banged and flapped over the mules' backs; tutor and pupils were boys once more, and simply shouted with delight as they clattered through the quiet streets. Much to his disgust the great Royds did not come in first. His was the worst mule, he explained at *table-d'hôte*.

All slept soundly that night at Martigny.

There they again fell in with the ladies of the hut on Montanvert, and talked, with all the energy of comrades in danger, of the crossing of the Mer de Glace and the descent of the Mauvais Pas, to the not-unreasonable amusement of Royds. Next morning they left for Brieg, going by rail to Sierre, not without missing the first train, and imprecating maledictions on the head of the landlord who, his hotel being somewhat empty, was constrained to adopt some measures for detaining his profitable guests. Arrived at Sierre, they were told the *diligence* for Brieg had started, and were offered carriages. A little patience, however, proved this to be one of the usual misrepresentations, and in due course, after a hearty *déjeûner* in the pretty old inn, they started in the company of a very fat ecclesiastic and a young and happy couple of Americans. From Brieg, which they reached at eight, after heavy rain, they were to ascend the Bel-alp, where Edwards intended to stay for a clear fortnight or three weeks for work.

There was no *diligence* to the Bel-alp; that they knew; but they had fondly hoped there was a carriage-road. They were quickly undeceived. There was only a bridle-path, and it was now late and getting dark. But Edwards had resolved to push on without further delay, and, seeing he was firm, the landlord of " La Poste " raised no objections. The heavier luggage was to be carried up, on the following day. The absolute necessaries were packed on the sturdy shoulders of two guides; and at half-past eight the party started. The rain, which had been falling heavily all the afternoon, fortunately ceased, but there was no moon, and the clouds hung thickly. The darkness intensified the grandeur of the hills and made the climb seem harder. Once, as they passed between a cluster of *chálets*, all dark and still, the moon struggled into view, and far below they saw a great white sea; but it was only the mist that lay along the valley. At half-past ten they reached the first halting-place, a little *chálet* perched on a level plateau. There was no light, and only the sound of the bells on the cows whose slumbers they had disturbed. But presently, after some patient knocking, the door was opened by a young giant of seven feet, with a sturdy girl at his side.

Royds, the officious, the experienced, the polite traveller, advanced, took off his hat, and made some remarks in French; but neither host nor hostess understood him, and the guide's *patois* was necessary to explain. In they all trooped to the rough, low, wooden room, glad enough to rest. The wine was sour, but it was the landlord's best; and they all made merry. Then one of the guides sang a Tyrolese ditty, of which the following is a paraphrase :—

> " With rifle aye ready,
>   A dog of sharp scent,
> And a maiden to love him,
>   A lad is content.
>
> " What needs hath the hunter?
>   The hunter hath none
> But a nut-brown-eyed maiden,
>   A dog, and a gun.
>
> " On Sunday, the church-day,
>   To dance we are gone;
> Andrew leads Peggy,
>   Janet leads John."

And then the guides, the landlord, and his wife

all sang together; the young giant representing the love-sick tenor in such a way as to make every one shout with laughter :—

Tenor.	" Out of the Tyrol I come, a long, long way,
	To look for my sweetheart, my little May.
Bass.	What does he say ?
Soprano.	Ah, poor lover !
All.	So long, so long he has not seen his love,
	So long he has not seen his love !
Tenor.	" As any bright penny was my little Jenny !
	And a dimple was in
	My Jenny's sweet chin !
Bass.	What does he say ?
All.	So long, so long he has not seen his love
Tenor.	" 'Tis two long years agone
	Since I left my love alone ;
	I'd give my true love's weight in gold
	Could I her face behold.
Bass.	Hark what he says !
Soprano.	O what a fond lover !
All.	So long, so long he has not seen his love ! "

And then Edwards sang an English song, the rest joining in the chorus, to the infinite delight of the Switzers. After which the guide suggested moving on.

At half-past one they reached the Bel-alp, and found, somewhat to their surprise, that there was

no village, not even a *chalet*, but only a great inn,
half wooden, half stone. The landlord, a little,
fat, hoarse-speaking man, with a thick black
moustache, and two cow-girls, called chamber-
maids, with their faces swathed in flannel, met
them ; and presently they slept soundly in their
little bare rooms, with their wooden walls and
ceilings, that made them feel for all the world as
though they were dolls put to bed in boxes.

But what a view next morning ! Down there
in the valley, as they stand at the inn door, they
can just make out where Brieg lies. Beyond, the
entrance to the Simplon Pass ; and, over all, the
Matterhorn, Weisshorn, Monte Leone, Mischabel,
and the Fletschhorn. Up behind them towers
the great white Sparrenhorn. Down on the left
crawls the broad Aletsh Glacier, with its huge,
rough, pale-blue waves moving and melting, and
foaming at the " snout " in torrents of stormy
water.

The inn was full, and three weeks went pleasantly enough. People came and went, for the
most part bound to or from the Eggisch-horn.
Every now and then there was a brief excitement
caused by the arrival of some friend whom chance

had brought. Some of the visitors were regularly
settled, and with these the men soon formed
acquaintance: notably, Professor Tyndall, who
was there on one of his usual summer visits,
measuring the motion of the glaciers, and who, as
"Father of the Table-d'hôte," made the meals
doubly pleasant with his genial talk and merry
laugh. Then there was another, well known in
the public-school world, with his wife—a jolly
pair—and a young couple from Ireland, who,
oddly enough, turned out to be distant connexions
of Lang. The husband fraternized with the men
in their climbs. The wife spent most of her
time rambling along the mountain paths within
easy distance, in which she was not unfrequently
accompanied by Royds, who flattered himself on
being eminently a "ladies' man." There were
several old ladies who, each evening, used
to entice the men to whist. Frank usually
was one of those caught. Lang and Maude,
the two lazy ones of the party, always retired to the smoking-room, whence they never
emerged till midnight. The others, for the most
part, read in the common sitting-room. Edwards
devoted four hours in the morning to his pupils'

1

work, from 8 to 12, and one hour before dinner. Out of respect for Lang and Maude, their
hour was fixed at 11. But, as often as not,
when that hour arrived, on looking out of the
window to call them in, their coach would hear
that they were not down yet, or would see
them strolling casually down the hill to meet the
mules which brought the letters or the day's pro-
visions from Brieg.

"Haven't got any work ready yet," would be
Lang's answer, if Edwards managed to overtake
them.

"Do you mind taking me after dinner?" from
Maude.

But in spite of the idleness of these two, the
average amount of work achieved by the party
was very creditable, and Edwards was satisfied.

At the end of the fixed three weeks, to the great
regret of the landlord (for he found the young
Oxonians thirsty to a degree) and of most of the
guests, the party departed. They went as they
came, on foot, with a couple of horses to carry
their luggage, and a couple of guides to carry
Lang, who had contrived to strain his ankle.
They slept one night in Brieg—a short, restless

night, with the *diligences* rolling through the streets and clattering into the courtyards, with jingling bells and cracking whips, the shouts of the drivers, and the agonized voices of weary and confused travellers. At six, in the fresh clear dawn, they took the *diligence* for the Rhone Glacier, and thence over the Furka to Andermatt. There, also, they slept one night—in fact, slept so soundly that when the *diligence* started next morning for Flüelen by the St. Gothard Pass, Edwards, Frank, and Royds alone were in time for breakfast and for choice of seats; Hoskins and Kingdon only saved their seats by chasing the *diligence* after it had started; while the first that Lang and Maude saw of the morning was the sight of the *diligence* turning a corner, with three of their companions seated outside, and two running frantically after it. But they consoled themselves with the reflection that this delay would furnish them with an excellent excuse for " cutting " the next day's lesson with Edwards. Frank was separated from the rest of the party, having for his companion a little soldier who spoke neither French nor German, but an unintelligible *patois* which made conversation impossible.

About ten o'clock they passed Altdorf. The little town looked so bright and gay, full of reverence for its William Tell, and ignorant of, or despising, the knowledge that makes his story a myth. Thence to Flüelen, and thence over the clear waters of the Vierwaldstätter See to Lucerne. What a change from the Bel-alp! Here all is softened—grown Italian almost. Just in the distance a few snowy peaks; but the frowning heights have melted to soft wooded hills—running down to look at themselves in the glassy mirror. Lucerne was reached about one o'clock; and here, at the Englischer Hof, right on the quay, a hospitable welcome met them.

Lang and Maude revelled in the change. For them the Bel-alp was too cold, too dull; but here they had the lake, the shops, the *cafés*, the band at night, and all those countless charms which no English town seems to possess. Here even Frank relaxed a little. They made excursions every day, for the most part in the comfortable little steamers. They went up the Rigi luxuriously in the train. Edwards, Royds, and Frank climbed Pilatus; the rest were content with the Rigi. They bought presents, useless as well as useful; they strummed on the *salon* piano, and sang in broken German, to the intense delight of the waiters. They spent the evenings invariably in a little *café* round the corner, where Gretchen's merry black eyes flashed from one to another, hardly divining the relationship of the party; or, if not there, on the *boulevard*, listening to the band; and sometimes on the lake; and it was on one of these occasions that Edwards astonished them by his vocal as well as his poetical powers.

He called his song, "The Lay of the Vice-Chancellor," and it ran as follows :—

"I've sung you many a ditty, some stupid and some witty,
  In our snug and cosy common-rooms after dinner many a day ;
But there's one I have omitted, of a blunder I committed,
  That may serve you as a warning, and may while an hour away.
When I was young and hearty, I took a reading party
              ("Hear, hear!" from the audience)
To study in America one summer long ago ;
And while out there we tarried, I went—and—I got married,
  And what that is, my bachelors, you very little know.
But upon that little portion of my most unhappy tale,
Will you kindly, will you kindly draw a veil, draw a veil?
    Chorus.—Draw a veil! draw a veil!

" But oh ! when I reflected that I should be expected
　　To forfeit either Fellowship or wife,
I thought 'twould be a pity she should leave her native city
　　And be tied to an old tutor all her life.
When I pictured you all cosy, at your port wine old and rosy,
　　And I was at cold mutton, and romance was growing cool—
When I thought of you so gaily dining gloriously daily,
　　I took a *single* cabin in a ship for Liverpool.
But upon the mix'd emotions of my hurried homeward sail,
Will you kindly, will you kindly draw a veil, draw a veil ?
　　Chorus (*very gently*).—Draw a veil ! draw a veil !

" Since then, by her unhamper'd, up fame's ladder I have
　　　　scamper'd,
　　And run through all our snug berths in a trice ;
I've been Bursar, Dean, Professor, Public Orator, Assessor,
　　And sat on a commission once or twice.
I've told quite different stories to the Liberals and Tories ;
　　I've snarl'd among the Radicals, " Retrench ! "
But I really should not wonder if my friend Lord Blood-and-
　　　　Thunder,
　　On the very next occasion, should transfer me to the Bench.
So really let me beg you on *that* portion of my tale,
Will you kindly, will you kindly draw a veil, draw a veil ?
　　Chorus.—Draw a veil ! draw a veil !

When they were all back again in Oxford, even
many terms afterwards, " Draw a veil " was always
a sort of pass-word between them.

A fortnight soon passed, and they travelled together to Paris.　Here they parted, Frank going

straight to Porchester, Edwards to Oxford. Frank had made a good start with his law reading, and, thanks to Edwards' style of teaching, had thoroughly grasped all that he had touched, and what is more, liked his subjects. One practical point before passing to other scenes: his expenses were 50*l*.;—35*l*. for railway fares, hotel bills, &c., 15*l*. to Edwards for tuition.

CHAPTER VIII.

IN THE THICK OF IT.

PAUL'S had no Law Lecturers, and Frank was therefore compelled to "put on a coach." He accordingly wrote to Edwards, a week before term commenced, to arrange with him. Much to his surprise, the College offered to pay half the fee on his behalf, which after all was but fair, considering that he had to pay his College tuition fees, although there were no lectures for him. By Edwards' advice he attended certain of the Law Professors' Lectures, which were open to the University at large—in some cases on payment of 1*l.*, in others free. Six hours in each week were spent at these, and three hours with Edwards; and with a daily average of four hours' private reading he considered he was industrious. His degree seemed so far off. He would work more when the time was drawing nearer. So he consoled himself, and so the time went by.

Of Crawford he saw little, for it was his last term, and he was in for Honours in the Final Classical Schools in November. But on Sunday they used to lunch together—alternately in one another's rooms—and go for a long constitutional afterwards. To Crawford alone of his many friends he confided his hopes. To him alone he told his dreams of Rose, of their engagement, and even of the marriage in the future. And Crawford never laughed at him, or pooh-poohed the notion as a boyish fancy; for he saw that if there was one thing more than another which would keep him straight, and make him stick to his work, it was the hope of one day making a home for Rose. But the Bar! How hopeless it seemed! To talk of marriage, at least three years before the wig could be worn, much less a brief gained! Still the boy was hopeful. And why damp his energy? Besides, Crawford had a belief—he knew it was not a prevalent one—that though there are so many barristers, the Bar as a profession is not really so crowded as the world believes; that if you eliminate the large numbers of so-called barristers who live by their pen, by speculating—by anything, in fact, except the

profession they claim, the number of men left
is by no means large enough to do the work that
offers.   Again, he knew that he came of a
family of lawyers, with large firms in various
towns, and at least one of considerable eminence
in London.   So that altogether he by no
means considered the boy's ambitions and dreams
as baseless or silly.   As for himself, he hardly
cared to confess his hopes.   But Frank had always
placed him, in anticipation, in the position Crawford secretly desired.   He seemed fitted in every
way for a Fellowship and Tutorship.   To begin
with, he was a gentleman in birth and in heart.
He would therefore know how to feel with, and
for, all the various grades of men with whom
he would come in contact : unlike the many
who, with neither the breeding nor the feelings
of gentlemen, have nothing but their intellectual supremacy to recommend them.

As to Crawford's intellectual powers, he had
already given ample proof.   He had taken a first
class in Classical Moderations.   He had won
the Chancellor's prize for Latin Verse, and had
been *proxime accessit* for the Stanhope Essay.
And then, to crown all, from the boyish under-

graduate point of view, he had rowed in his College Eight, and won the Diamond Sculls at Henley. Why, he was the very *beau-ideal* of a Fellow. A handsome, clever, athletic English gentleman. Oxford has had many such, and, thank God, she has them still. Men who consider a fellowship and tutorship a sacred trust; who look upon the undergraduates as friends to be helped, guided, and taught, but not in mere learning for the schools; who will draw out, not crush, the fresh hopefulness of youth; who will cheer, not cloud, boys' ambitions; who will look for good qualities, not watch and wait for errors; whose chief thought will be what good they can do, and not what fines they can impose.

"Do you see much of Monkton now?" Crawford asked, as they were walking to Godstow by the upper river.

"Very little," said Frank. "I can't think what he does with himself."

"Not much, I fancy. I see him loafing occasionally, and I believe that's pretty nearly all he does. However, I'm glad you don't see much of him." And Crawford changed the subject. "What's this I hear of you and the *Undergraduates'*

Journal? You don't mean to say you've taken to write in it? I should have thought you had work enough to do."

Frank got red and confused.

" Well, the fact is—I have written a few things; but it didn't take much time."

" Ah! that's just where it is," said Crawford. " If you do anything of that sort at all, it's worth doing well—just as everything is, for the matter of that. You haven't time to do it well, and you square the matter by doing it hurriedly. You'd far better stick to your Law reading."

"I say, old fellow," remonstrated Frank, "I didn't come out for a lecture. You're a regular old school-master. I only wrote three little poems, or 'sets of verses' as I suppose I ought to call'em: that's the extent of my writing."

" Oh!" said Crawford, somewhat mollified. " Well, take my advice; get your degree first and write afterwards."

" That's all very well," retorted Frank; "but I should like to know how you expect a fellow to be able to write without practice? Reading Law and writing answers to papers don't help one."

" I don't think we'll discuss the question any

further," answered Crawford. "You want to marry Rose, I know, as quickly as possible. Well, my opinion is that you'll do it a great deal more quickly by reading Law than by writing poetry."

Frank was silent. There was truth in what Crawford said, he knew; but he could not help writing poetry. And whether he will ever be a known poet, ever succeed in charming the hydra-headed public, or not, he certainly had one requisite in a maker—spontaneity. Rose, of course, considered him a poet in the highest sense of the term. In fact, she cared for no poetry but his, which speaks volumes for her affection, but little for her powers of criticism. But if lovers are to be critics, Love may as well go to Mr. Critchet, and be operated on for cataract.

Term, with all its activity, was passing quickly. Every day till two o'clock Frank devoted himself to his work. From two till five he rowed, or practised at the butts. From five till six he usually spent at the Union, reading the papers or magazines. Dinner at six. He did not do much work in the evening, for various reasons—chiefly, because he was too lazy—excusing himself because he thought his eyes were weak; and partly because of various engagements. On Tuesday evening there was either a regular Apollo lodge-meeting, or a lodge of instruction. Monday, the Paul's Debating Society. Wednesday, the practice of the Philharmonic, a somewhat different form of excitement from the usual undergraduate amusements, owing to the presence of a large number of ladies. Thursday, the debate at the Union, in which he usually took part. Friday and Saturday had no definite fixture; but then there was always something in the shape of nondescript entertainment at the "Vic.," or concert at the Town Hall or Corn Exchange; or else there was a friend to be asked to dinner in Hall, or an invitation to dinner to accept. Altogether, his evening work never amounted to more than one hour on the average.

One evening, seeing a large poster announcing a performance by "the great Bounce," he turned up the narrow little passage which leads from Magdalen Street to the "gaff" that is dignified by the name of theatre. Here, by permission of the Very Reverend the Vice-Chancellor, and his Worship the Mayor—a permission always necessary and always publicly announced—entertain-

ments of every description, as long as they are
not stage plays,. are performed. Conjurors,
mimics, ventriloquists, mesmerists, Tyrolese
singers, Japanese acrobats, music-hall singers
of every grade and degree, display themselves
before a crowded audience of undergraduates.
But anything so demoralizing as a play of
Shakespeare or other healthy author is strictly
forbidden. The authorities doubtless have their
reasons, but it is somewhat hard to imagine what
those reasons can be. An occasional concert
is given in the Town Hall or Corn Exchange,
to which of course ladies can go; but from
the entertainments in the "Vic.," good, bad,
or indifferent, they are absolutely debarred. And
in very, very few instances do they miss anything
worth seeing.

The first person whom Frank recognized on
entering was Monkton, who was sitting in a
stage-box, or at least in what does duty for a
stage-box. He was dressed in a somewhat
startling costume of ginger-colour check; a
bright crimson necktie; his hat well on the side
of his head; an enormous cigar in his mouth,
which he appeared to be sucking rather than

smoking. Between his knees, a gigantic bull-dog, whose efforts to plunge upon the stage or into the orchestra he was with difficulty control-ling. Another man sat with him, dressed, if it were possible, in louder style than he; and from the tone of their voices they appeared not a little pleased with themselves and with the impression they were creating. The theatre was crammed from floor to ceiling; the University element decidedly predominating; the town being repre-sented by a gallery full of that peculiar style of cad and cadger for which Oxford seems so famous. The smoke from pipes and cigars was far too thick to allow of recognition except at a very short distance; and Frank was much relieved to find that Monkton did not "spot" him.

We need not describe the performance. The vulgar, strutting, swaggering comique, who supplies in fancied wit what he lacks in voice; the booming tenor, who yells "Tom Bowling" to give respectability to the entertainment; the brazen-throated "lady vocalist," who disdains to be called a singer, and who certainly doesn't deserve the title, are all too wearisome and

sickening to merit notice, but for the lamentable
fact that they are patronized by the undergraduate because the University authorities refuse
to sanction anything better.

The entertainment had not proceeded very far
before Monkton had attracted the notice of the
" star " of the evening, who, seeing that he had
the audience on his side, commenced, in the
spoken portion of his performance, to chaff " the
gentleman in ginger." Monkton's position was
too prominent for him to venture to respond;
perhaps, too, he was not good at repartee. At
all events, he drew back out of sight as far as
possible, contenting himself with allowing his
dog to put his forefeet on the cushion of the box
and to growl an answer to the chaff.

The next performer happened to be a young
lady not quite so much at her ease as is usual in
these persons. She was evidently frightened at
the dog; and Monkton, seeing his opportunity,
made the brute growl and spring forward as near
the singer as possible. There were loud cries of
" Turn him out !" The singer stopped in the
middle of her song, burst into tears, and ran off
at the wings. The manager came forward and

K

expostulated. By this time the gallery was
infuriated. Then Monkton let the dog go, and
with a bound he cleared the orchestra and leapt
on the stage. The manager, in evident trepida-
tion, rushed off. The orchestra seized their
instruments, and hastily began to decamp; some
one in the confusion turned out most of the gas;
and at that moment a cry of "Proctors!" was
heard.

It was by the merest chance that the Senior
Proctor happened to be passing, and hearing the
unusual disturbance, and the shouts which were
evidently not shouts of applause, came in. He
sent two of his men to one door, and he himself
with two waited at the principal exit. There
they took everybody's "name and College,"
giving directions as to the usual call on the
following morning; and then, when the theatre
was emptied, sent for the manager, and learned
the facts of the case. Monkton had, of course,
made his way out with the rest, with no further
notice from the Proctor than they; but his time
was to come.

There was a great crowd at nine the next
morning at the Senior Proctor's rooms. The

men went as a matter of form, hardly expecting to be fined for going to an entertainment sanctioned by the University, and simply anticipating an order to attend before the Vice-Chancellor for an investigation of the *fracas* of the preceding evening. Monkton appeared with the rest; and from the way in which every one gave him the cold shoulder he saw pretty clearly that no one would screen him. At twelve o'clock he received an official notice to answer before the Vice-Chancellor to the charge of setting and inciting a bulldog, with intent to do bodily injury, and so forth.

At eleven o'clock on the following day there was such a crowd as had not been seen in the Vice-Chancellor's Court for many a long day. The case was investigated as before a magistrate, the Vice-Chancellor being *ex officio* a justice of the peace for the city of Oxford, with, however, far greater powers. There were plenty of undergraduates who gave evidence in support of the charge, and the manager and singers gladly exonerated the rest of the audience. It was acknowledged on all sides that neither Monkton nor the "star" comique put in so easy and unembarrassed an appearance before the Very Reverend the Vice-Chancellor and the Proctors as they did in their respective positions on the eventful evening. It was in vain that Monkton's solicitor urged provocation on the part of the "star." There were plenty of men ready to testify that they too had been chaffed. The Vice-Chancellor gave the defendant a sharp reprimand, fined him 5*l.*, and " sent him down for a term."

The Proctor's summons to the rest of the men was allowed to pass, and they heard no more of the matter.

The Michaelmas Law Term commenced on the 2nd of November, and Frank obtained leave from the Dean to go to town to enter at the Inner Temple and eat his first three dinners. He left at 9 a.m., with feelings somewhat akin to those he had on starting from home for matriculation, with the important difference, however, that there was no examination to face. His father met him at Paddington, and they drove straight to the Temple. At the gate of the " Inner " they found the two friends who had promised to be sureties for the payment of fees. With them they went to the Steward's office, and there Frank presented a paper signed by the Dean of Paul's to the effect

that he had passed a Public Examination at
Oxford. This exempted him from any examination on admission as a student of the Inns of
Court. On payment of one guinea he obtained a
form of admission, to be signed by two barristers
to vouch for his respectability, with which he and
his father went to the chambers of two friends,
who gave the necessary signatures; then back
again to the Treasurer's office, where the two
sureties entered into a bond to the amount of
50*l.*; and by a further payment of five guineas for
the privilege of attending the Public Lectures
of the Law Professors, and 35*l.* 6*s.* 5*d.* for fees
and stamp on admission, the whole business was
complete, and Frank was a student of the Honourable Society of the Inner Temple.

A little pleasant chaff about the woolsack, and
the quartet broke up, the two sureties to their
respective businesses, Frank and his father to
lunch. Then Mr. Ross took a cab to Paddington,
leaving Frank at the door of Maskelyne and
Cooke's mysterious entertainment, where he proposed a little mild dissipation till it was time to
go down to the Temple to dine.

Hurrying through the crowd of students and

newspaper-boys at the lodge just before six o'clock, he met three friends, and the usual expressions of mutual surprise were uttered. They agreed to make up a mess together, and certainly would not have accepted the definition of a mess as "a party of four who eye each other with feelings of mutual distrust and suspicion." Frank, as freshman, had to "stand" the orthodox bottle of wine, and felt quite like an old fogey as he "took wine" with the three. With the exception of wine, and the power of sending for various sorts of liquors, the dinner was very much the same as the usual dinner in Hall at Oxford. The servants were better dressed, but waited worse. There was more order, from the fact that everybody has to be present at grace before and after meat, failing which, the dinner does not count. Then the diversity of age and style of men struck Frank. Old men and beardless boys sitting side by side, wearing the student's gown; mild-looking students with pale faces and spectacles: fast men, in whom the notion of study seemed a ridiculous anomaly; dark faces from the East; and even a few of the thick lips from Africa. All the rest—the Benchers at the high table, the portraits overhead, the coloured windows, the fretted roof, the carved panelling—it was all familiar; Oxford over again, simply transplanted to the very heart of London.

After dinner they went to a theatre, and after that Frank was initiated into the mysteries of Evans's.

The three evenings passed all too quickly, and he was once more in Oxford, with the sense of having at least made one distinct step towards winning Rose, even though it was such a matter-of-fact affair as the eating of three dinners.

There was not much to mark the succeeding Lent Term. There were the " Torpids " as usual, in which Frank again rowed, and with such decided improvement that he was considered safe for the " Eight " in the summer term. There was the ordinary scarlet-fever scare ; a suicide of a studious undergraduate, the annual result of the climate, and the Lenten depression of the social atmosphere ; and there were the Christ-Church Grinds,[1] and the Brasenose Ale Festival on Shrove Tuesday.

[1] Steeplechases.

To the former Frank went, surreptitiously of course, for the Grinds are with annual regularity forbidden, but with equal regularity carried out. The Proctors for the time being were not over-sharp, and imagined that the simplest and easiest way to catch the men coming home from Ayles-bury was to go to the station and meet the in-trains. But, strange to relate, not a single un-dergraduate was to be found! Innocently con-fessing his failure on the following evening in Common Room, the Senior Proctor drew upon himself the ridicule of one of the older fellows, a sporting man, and the " inextinguishable laugh-ter " of the rest.

" You don't mean to say you expected to find them at the station ? Why, man alive ! what is easier than to tip the guard and engine-driver half-a-sovereign, and have the train stopped just by the Goods-station ? "

The Senior Proctor mentally resolved to be sharper in future. He was sharper—when he caught men. But his sharpness was the sharpness of acidity and not of acuteness.

The Brasenose Ale Festival is simply ordinary dinner in Hall, at which some special ale, brewed

by the College and kept for high occasions, is
given in unlimited quantities to the undergraduates. Possibly the most important feature (certainly it is the most uncommon) is the fact of
the ale being given. Anything not paid for is a
fact so rare that of itself it deserves a festival
to commemorate it. The ale is celebrated in a
poem which is supposed to be written by the
College Butler. College Butlers being, however,
not necessarily gifted with the poetic faculty, the
honour or duty is deputed to some undergraduate.
The merits of the verses vary, apparently with
the quality of the ale, which is sometimes good,
often bad, and usually indifferent. In a collection
of the productions of the laureates of the barrel,
lately published, are verses by Bishop Heber, by
Garbett, once Professor of Poetry, and others of
less reputation. The various later authors may be
found in country rectories, doubtless endeavour-
ing on temperance principles to counteract the
effects of the obnoxious liquor, which in the days
of their youth they celebrated in such festive
fashion.

The College bounty did not stop short, however,
at ale; cakes of ample proportions were cut up

and distributed. But when all rose to bless the indirect giver, and the direct benefactor, it must of course have been indigestion or malicious scepticism which made Frank's host whisper to him,—

"I wonder what the difference is between the pecuniary value of the bequest, when it was made to the College, and its present value."

Frank, not being able to hazard a conjecture, made the most apposite remark his state of ignorance allowed,—

"You'd better ask the Bursar."

CHAPTER IX.

THE CLOSE.

FRANK read with Edwards in the Summer term, the College again paying half the fee. He rowed in the Eights, and Paul's made four bumps, thereby getting head of the river. To commemorate the event a "bump-supper" was given. All the men, with the exception of a very few, subscribed the necessary guinea, and, as many brought guests, the supper was emphatically a success. The exceptions were of the three ordinary types: those who could not afford a guinea for such a purpose, and who were not ashamed to say so; those who considered "bump-suppers" and such-like entertainments as immoral orgies; and lastly, those who both enjoyed them and who could afford to subscribe, but who were too mean to do so, and preferred rather to extract an invitation to another college bump-supper in the specious manner which

usually characterizes the tight-fingered. The
Dons readily gave permission for the use of the
hall, with certain provisos as to time of termina-
tion of the feast. Cooks and scouts vied with one
another, in a spirit not altogether disinterested,
in supplying and laying out the best that the
College kitchen could provide. A gorgeous
dessert was ordered from a neighbouring con-
fectioner, and wine came in without stint or stay.
Slap's[1] excellent band was engaged, and dis-
coursed most sweet music from time to time
during the evening. And then, what speeches
were made! What songs were sung! How
they all cheered when the captain of the boat-club
returned thanks! And—tell it not in the Common
Room, whisper it not to the Dons (for the very
simple reason that they know by experience what
it all means)—what aching eyes, what cracking
heads, what foul and furry tongues there were
next morning! Nor did the store of College
legends fail to receive the additions usual on such
occasions; and one story even reached the
Master's ears: how that the captain of the boat-

[1] Affectionate abbreviation for Slapoffski, unrivalled in
Oxford, and not unknown outside.

club was observed, long after the last guest had
passed the porter's lodge, sitting in a corner of
one of the back quadrangles, rowing with all his
might at an imaginary oar, shouting every now
and then to "bow" to keep time, and telling the
"cox" not to put the rudder on so sharp).

Frank did not stay up for Commemoration;
that he reserved as a pleasure for the following
year. His final examination would then be over,
and he would be able to enjoy all the fun
and gaiety in his new glory as Bachelor of
Arts. Before going down he had a consultation
with Edwards as to his work in the "Long."
The latter was again going to take a reading
party abroad, but he advised Frank not to join;
he told him that in his present state of progress
he could do more work at home. Frank was
relieved by the advice, for he knew his father
could not afford to send him abroad again. But
he felt he might close with Edwards' proposal to
come up a month before the Michaelmas Term
began, chiefly for the purpose of making his work
safe for the first Bar Examination in Roman Law,
which was fixed for the end of October. Edwards
wished him to go in for this on his first oppor-

tunity; for he felt that, apart from the direct advantage in passing, the examination would prove of service as a partial test for the final Oxford Examination in the ensuing summer.

Mr. Ross was not only satisfied but pleased with the scheme for Frank's work. He was a man who always looked ahead and tried to map out the future. He felt that men for the most part create their own future, and that where the object in view is clearly marked out, and the means to that object carefully weighed and chosen with firm determination, chance is but a trifling factor in a man's career. He loathed that comfortable philosophy which folds its hands and leaves "Time and the hour" to work for one. So far his plans had been fulfilled; and if this had made him somewhat dogmatic and obstinately fond of insisting that "anything can be done if only there is the will to do it," it had, at all events, taught his children the lesson of dogged perseverance and the value of far-sightedness.

Frank spent a pleasant "Long" vacation. He had plenty of cricket and boating; he saw Rose at least three times every week. There were endless picnics and lawn-tennis parties. Above

all, he got through a good deal of reading. During
the three months he was at home he worked,
on an average, five hours every day; but by
judiciously arranging these he always found
plenty of time for amusements. He bathed in
the river, wet or fine, every morning at seven;
read from eight till nine; breakfasted at nine;
read from ten till one. By this plan he always had
done four hours' work before luncheon; and he
had no difficulty in keeping up his average number
by regulating the rest of his work according to
the general plans for the day's amusements.

The month's reading in Oxford during the
" Long " was, of course, a novelty, but he did not
find the dulness he expected. He saw a good
deal more of Edwards than in his tutorial capacity,
and soon made great friends with his wife; and
as young men are at a premium in Oxford out of
term, his social vanity was flattered by numerous
invitations.

Towards the latter part of October he went to
town for the Bar Examination. He put up at the
Inns of Court Hotel, to be near Lincoln's Inn, in
the Hall of which he duly appeared one Saturday
morning at ten o'clock. He saw plenty of familiar

faces and several friends. One of the examiners also was an Oxford professor. The paper—there only was one—was not difficult, and Frank had very nearly finished when, just on the stroke of twelve o'clock, he was called up for *vivâ voce.* The plan struck him as strange; and as he was kept waiting for at least twenty minutes, he envied the other candidates who were still writing or looking over their papers. His *vivâ voce,* however, did not last very long, and he had ample time to correct his work carefully. Within a week he received the pleasant news that he had passed, and went up in November to eat his dinners, with a certain amount of pride at having achieved one more distinct step towards his desired end.

Not long after this, Crawford, who had taken a "first" in the summer, gained a Fellowship at Queen's; and by an odd coincidence, another of his friends, Monkton, was sent down about the same time. His rustication after the escapade in the theatre had apparently failed to inspire him with any awe of the University authorities, and he had scorned the notion of the Proctors being able to track or catch him in any of his favourite haunts, till one night he received palpable and painful evidence to the contrary. The matter was promptly settled. He was summoned before the Vice-Chancellor and the Proctors privately; his previous offence was proved against him; a bad report came from his own college authorities; his name was removed from the books, and he was told to leave Oxford at once. The remainder of his history is neither poetic nor uncommon. He disappeared from the surface for a season, only to rise, however, on the tide of a theological college. Thence, having easily satisfied a bishop—for he was by no means a fool—he was ordained, and, having passed a few years as junior curate, was promoted to be his vicar's vicegerent, and glided into a more comfortable, decent existence, much invited and much beslippered by the ladies of his congregation.

The spring soon passed away, and with the end of May all the examinations began.

Frank felt far more nervous when he appeared in the Schools for Divinity than subsequently for Law. Failure in the former would prevent him from taking his degree that term; and failure was quite possible even to one who had a very good

general knowledge of the matter and teaching of
the Bible. It is not easy to see what good is
effected by an examination which induces cram-
ming, irreverence, and a cordial dislike of its
subject. It certainly furnishes an inexhaustible
store of amusing stories.

" *What do you know of Gamaliel ?* "

"It is a mountain in Syria."

" *Who was Mary Magdalene ?* "

" The mother of our Lord."

" *Who was Zacchæus ?* "

" He was the man who climbed up a sycamore-
tree, exclaiming, 'If they do these things in the
green tree, what will they do in the dry ? ' "

" *Describe accurately the relations between the
Jews and Samaritans from the earliest periods.*"

" The Jews had no dealings with the Samaritans."

" *What is the meaning of phylactery ?* "

" An establishment where love-philtres were
made. The Pharisees did a good business in
these; hence the expression ' Make broad your
phylacteries,' means, " Extend your business.' "

" *Why was our Lord taken before the high priest
first, and not before Pilate ?*"

" Because Peter had cut off his servant's ear."

" *Who was Malchus ?* "

" He was the high priest's servant whose ear Peter cut off, and supposed to be the author of a treatise on population."

Frank contributed one to the stock of blunders. Given the Greek words and asked to explain the context of " The thorns sprang up and choked it," he translated them, "The thieves sprang up and choked him ;" and proceeded to give an elaborate description of the parable of the Good Samaritan. He did not, however, end in the legendary manner : " He took out two pence and gave them to the host, saying, ' Whatsoever thou spendest more, when I come again I will repay thee.' This he said, well knowing he should see his face no more."

He answered the rest of the paper, as he thought, fairly ; and, from the short *viva voce* he had a few days later, inferred that the written part of his work was better than he imagined ; and two hours afterwards received in exchange for the customary shilling the much-coveted piece of blue paper from the patient Parker, clerk of the schools. A few days elapsed, and then he went in for Law. We need not follow him through all the details. As so often happens, he did better than he expected in the subjects he feared most, and worse in those he fancied. he should do better. But on the whole he was satisfied with his performance. In *vivâ voce* he considerably improved his position, and to this he attributed the fact that when the class-list appeared he found himself in the second instead of the third class. A first he had never expected to get; but Edwards learnt from the examiners that he was considered a good second-class man, having amply retrieved in *vivâ voce* the failure in one of his papers which had threatened to lower him to the third.

CHAPTER X.

GOWN AT LAST.

So now it was all over—all the work and anxiety. The taking of his degree remained, and—Commemoration. It was Thursday when the class-list appeared. The following Sunday was Show Sunday, the semi-official commencement of the festivities. He telegraphed to his father: " Have got a second. You must come up for Commem. I hope to put on my gown on Thursday." He telegraphed to Rose. He wrote a long letter to his mother by that night's post, begging her to bring one of his sisters and Rose. He wrote to Rose herself. He was in a whirl of excitement, and to conceal his emotion he ordered an elegant summer suit, which he did not in the least require, at a most obliging tailor's not a hundred yards from St. Mary's Church. So obliging was he, in fact, that it is matter of history

that when a certain wealthy and aristocratic Irish-
man, in a flow of unbounded extravagance, ordered him to " send in his whole shop," the tailor,
with undisturbed equanimity, replied, " Certainly,
sir !   What time would you like it ? "

The receipt of Frank's letter, and the request
that his mother would bring Rose, produced a
little commotion.   His father still tried to pooh-
pooh the notion of an engagement ; but his mother,
who had Frank's confidence, maintained that, as
far as the two were concerned, the engagement
was a reality, and that it only waited the formal
consent of the parents and the means to marry.
So it was at last decided that Mr. and Mrs. Ross,
and Frank's elder sister, Mary, would go.   The
Vicar, glad of an excuse to visit Oxford again,
agreed to join the party and bring Rose.   And
Rose herself—well, there was no need to ask her
consent.   On Friday morning a telegram was
despatched to Frank, telling him they were coming
on Saturday evening, and giving him directions
to secure lodgings ; and Mary and Rose were together most of the day and evening, arranging,
selecting, altering, and making various articles of
adornment for the coming gaieties.

Pembroke concert had taken place on Thursday, Queen's on Friday, and there was nothing for Saturday. But that was no loss to Frank's party, for they were all too tired for any gaiety after their long journey. By a fluke—for he was late in looking for lodgings—he found some disengaged rooms in Grove Street; and the shady little corner, so close to the sunny, busy High, was most pleasant and convenient. After supper the Vicar went down to Christ-Church to "look up" some old friends, still in residence as Senior Students,[1] and the rest strolled by Merton to the river. Mr. and Mrs. Ross, not caring to trust themselves to the boat which Frank had chosen, wandered round the paths by the Cherwell, and, after losing themselves by the Botanical Gardens, eventually got safe to Grove Street. Frank rowed Rose and Mary down to Sandford, where he gave them tea in the little inn overlooking the lock, and then took them round to see the lasher that has been so fatal to many bright young lives.

Coming home, he pointed out to them all the

---

[1] Senior Students at Christ-Church correspond to Fellows at other Colleges.

spots of interest and importance to the rowing man. The tavern at Iffley where the last of the Eights starts in the races; the Green Barge, at the entrance to the "Gut;" the Gut itself, that terror of young coxswains; the Long Bridges; the White Willow where the boats make their final crossing to the Berkshire bank on the journey home. Every spot had its little history. Here, in the first Torpids, he had nearly "caught a crab." There his crew had made their final "spirt;" here they had bumped Brasenose, when the coxswain would not acknowledge the bump. There "bow" broke his oar, and nearly pitched out of the boat. Yonder, strolling quietly down the Berkshire bank, was Harvey, the Humane Society's man. There was old George West on the Brasenose barge; there, just above, was Timms, the "Father of the Crews," leading a quiet time of it, now that the "Eights" and the "Sculls" and "Pairs"[2] were over. Frank took the girls into the 'Varsity barge, and showed them the pictures of the old "oars," who had rowed for Oxford at Henley and Putney; and told them what little legends had come down to him

[2] *I. e.* races for sculling-boats and pair-oars.

of Chitty and Meade-King, Arkell and Warre,
Morrison and Woodgate; and, coming to later
times, of Tinney, Willan, Yarborough, and Dar-
bishire, the famous four who, besides their glories
at Putney, licked the Yankees from Harvard;
and, in later times still, of Leslie and Houblon,
Edwards-Moss and Marriott. They were all heroes
to Frank—these " brutal rowing men," as Mr.
Wilkie Collins deems them—these savages whose
only glory is their brute strength. It has been said
that English battles have been won in the Eton
playing-fields. Possibly the Isis and the Cam
have as much as anything to do with the feats of
dogged endurance and quiet pluck that have made
Alma and Inkerman, Isandula and Rorke's Drift,
immortal names in the annals of warfare.

On Sunday they all went to St. Mary's. The
Vicar's gown admitted the ladies to the seats
appropriated to the wives of the Masters of Arts,
and Mr. Ross to the seats of the Masters themselves. Frank, being still *de jure* an undergraduate, had to retire to the upstair gallery.
The church was crowded. People were even
standing in the aisles. The sermon, by a silver-
haired professor with a cherubic face, was a dis-

course on friendship, delivered, if somewhat monotonously, with a delicate utterance and in a delicate phraseology that was quite too charming; and if it formed a rather strange contrast to the anathemas thundered by rural Boanerges to placid congregations in sweltering country churches, the contrast was a pleasing one rather than otherwise.

"Well," said Mr. Ross as they emerged into the High, "that's an odd sort of sermon, eh, Vicar?"

Mr. Ross was a very sound lawyer, but he had not travelled much, nor had he heard many sermons other than those of his friend the Vicar. The Vicar smiled, and continued his explanations to Mrs. Ross of certain allusions to Oxford celebrities made by the preacher. Frank also, to whom his father appealed, had only a commonplace comment to make. His studies not having been philosophical, he could not go into raptures over every utterance of the new Plato.

The church was even more crowded, if that were possible, in the afternoon, in spite of the awkwardness of the hour (two o'clock) and the heat of the day. And what an assemblage of famous men was present! Gladstone and

Tyndall, Lord Selborne and Huxley, Forster and Sir Stafford Northcote, Sir William Harcourt and the Oxford Conservative member, all sitting amicably side by side, listening to one of those eloquent attacks on men of science which satisfy and please those for whom they are not needed, and only amuse those whom they are intended to convince.

After the sermon the Vicar and Mr. Ross betook themselves to the Union, to read the papers over a cup of coffee; and about a quarter to five Frank started with his mother, sister, and Rose, to Magdalen Chapel. Tickets had been, of course, difficult to get, and with all his exertions he had only been able to secure two for the choir, and two for the ante-chapel. The two former Mrs. Ross and Mary took, without any resistance, for they knew that Rose would be happier to be with Frank. How many husbands and wives come back in after-years to Oxford, to go over again all the old days, to revisit all the old spots, to find one particular tree the same, save, like themselves, a little older; to sit in the same chapel, and listen perhaps to the very same anthem they had listened to when they were boy and girl, sung by different voices, but for them the same; to pass the same surly porter, whose favour can only be purchased; to see the same placid gardener tidying up the velvet grass under the grey walls; to hear the same bells ringing; and, with it all, to feel as young as ever!

Frank and Rose, as they sat in the dim ante-chapel, under the great brown window that sheds such a strange light over all, thought neither of the past, for that was eclipsed, nor of the future, for that was uncertain, but just lived in the present. And if he did hold her hand during most of the service, nobody saw him, and therefore nobody's feelings were outraged.

Another happy pair emerged from another dim corner of the ante-chapel, when the service was over—Crawford and the little lady, who doubtless has not been forgotten, best known by the title "Blue-eyes." She, too, had in attendance on her a mother and sister; and they, too, had been sitting in the choir. So that altogether, when the introductions took place in the cloisters, all mentally agreed that the party was a most symmetrical one—two mothers, two sisters, and two pairs of lovers.

After dinner at their respective lodgings the two parties met in Grove Street, and went to the Broad Walk to see and contribute to the show of visitors. The Vicar pronounced a melancholy eulógium on the glories of past Show Sundays, from which the present was a sad falling-off, caused chiefly as he explained by the indiscriminate admission of the " Town," and the consequent absence of the " Gown " element. His hearers, however, having no historic past with which to contrast the present, though they listened submissively to his diatribes, enjoyed themselves immensely, stared at everybody, wondered, and questioned.

All the morning of Monday, Frank was engaged at a committee meeting of the Masonic Fête, of which he was a steward : and as he and one or two others were decidedly opposed to the general plan of disposal of tickets, the meetings were not so peaceable as hitherto; he used to return hot, tired, and annoyed. But Rose's presence soon restored him to his wonted equanimity.

On Monday afternoon there was a concert given by the Philharmonic Society in the Sheldonian Theatre, and after a hurried tea he took his

party to the river to see the procession of boats.
He had tickets for them for the 'Varsity barge,
and having got them good seats at the lower corner, next to the Brasenose barge, hurried off to
his own barge to put on his boating clothes. To
Rose and Mary, who had never seen any river-
boat except the " tubs " at Porchester, the long
slender craft were objects of much wonder,
and they thoroughly enjoyed the sight of the
many " Eights " and " Torpids " rowing up and
saluting Paul's, the head boat, which lay close
under the 'Varsity barge. The cox—a facetious
young gentleman—could not resist the pleasure
of shouting every few minutes, " Eyes in the
boat ! " as he caught the eyes of his crew wander-
ing to the many fair faces that were looking down
at them from beneath the awning.

One by one the boats rowed up—it is to be
feared not in the best style, for the crews were
for the most part mere " scratch " affairs got together hurriedly for the procession, in the absence
of the regular men who had gone down. One by
one they rowed up to the post opposite to the
'Varsity barge, " easied," and then, standing up,
raised their oars and saluted the head boat, " Well

rowed, Paul's!" to commemorate the honour of
the May races. Rose felt quite flattered, and took
to herself half the honour at least that was being
given to Frank's boat. The proceeding repeated
by some forty boats was growing somewhat mono-
tonous, when, to the intense delight and half-
terror of the ladies, one Eight upset—on purpose,
of course; and there was much merriment over
the intentionally assumed danger and frantic
efforts to get out of the crowded water. When
all the boats had saluted, they turned at Folly
Bridge (with what difficulty coxswains know to
their cost), and dropped down the stream to their
respective barges.

Those who embark on the festivities of Commemoration have not much time to spend in
dreaming. Rose would fain have gone down the
river quietly in the cool of the evening; and yet
—and yet—the thoughts of dancing were perhaps
sweeter.

Back to the town streamed the crowds: some
to the Wadham concert; some to rest before
dressing for the University ball; many to sum-
mon up their strength and energy for both.
Among the latter were Mrs. Ross and Mary, Rose

and Frank. The fathers dined at Christ-Church, and spent a cosy evening in the Common Room—the Vicar chatting away unceasingly with old friends, and Mr. Ross making a very pleasant and amused listener.

It was a lovely evening, and most of the people walked to Wadham—one of the many things that struck the country folks as strange and yet pleasant. The concert was held in the College Hall, beautifully decorated for the purpose. After the first part, every one adjourned to the gardens, where refreshments were served in a large tent, and then wandered about, enjoying the cool air till the second part began. Frank and his party did not return to the Hall, but went to the Corn Exchange, to the University ball. And what a night they had! He and Rose forgot to count how many times they danced together. Mary had partners in abundance, for Frank's friends were there in great force; and they were all longing for a dance with Rose, but had chiefly to console themselves with Mary, for Frank could not spare many dances. However, from Mary's happy face, as they walked down the High in the sweet early morning air, Frank inferred that the consoling process had been not unpleasant for all parties concerned.

Tuesday morning brought the much-needed rest, taken by some in chairs at home, by others in punts on the river (Frank and Rose preferred the latter). Tuesday afternoon—the flower-show held in the gardens of New College. A Commemoration flower-show is more than a flower-show. In fact, the flowers are almost the last thing regarded. Tuesday evening—New College concert, always one of the best, and the Masonic ball. Rose and Mary again in much request, but the former too deeply engaged to Frank to be able to spare many dances. To this ball Mr. Ross, being a Mason, went as a matter of course, and he even succeeded in enticing the Vicar. The latter had a lurking love of vestments, but Porchester gave him no encouragement; here, however, seeing the aprons and scarves, and the cloaks of the Templars, he thought he might satisfy his love. He would be a Mason, and though unable to disport himself in picturesque attire to his congregation in church, he might do so to his heart's content to his brethren in the secrecy of lodge-meetings, or the publicity of such a ball as

M

this. So strongly was he enamoured of the notion, that over supper, in a quiet corner with Mr. and Mrs. Ross, he asked that gentleman to propose him for election at a lodge in a town not far from Porchester, of which he was Worshipful Master.

Then came Wednesday, the day of Encænia, or Commemoration of the Founders and Benefactors. Who that has ever been present in the crowded Sheldonian Theatre can forget the scene? The jostling, pushing, squeezing that begins before ten o'clock, though the proceedings themselves seldom begin before noon; the pause and quiet, till the boldest undergraduate starts the chaff; the grave faces of the officials as they hand the ladies to their seats, half amused, half angry, when told by some wag in the gallery "not to squeeze her hand;" the cheers for everybody and everything that the occasion suggests—" the ladies in pink," " the ladies in blue," " the ladies who are engaged;" the groans for this statesman, the cheers for the other, for the 'Varsity Boat Club, the 'Varsity Eleven, the popular Proctors. Then the chaff becomes more personal. " When is the Vice-Chancellor coming ?" "Poor old man, he's nervous." " Has the Senior Proctor

gone to Aylesbury?" (alluding to the Christ-
Church grinds and the Senior Proctor's failure).
"*Dissolvimus hanc Convocationem*," uttered in
imitation of the Vice-Chancellor, and causing
much amusement among the Masters of Arts and
others familiar with the phrase. Just then a
very white-headed gentleman enters the area, and
is met with shouts of "White hat!" "Turn
him out!" For a long time the object of the
shouts is perfectly oblivious. At length he puts
on his hat, and is of course greeted with "Hats
off!" How long the uproar would have continued is hard to say, had not a huge paper fool's-
cap, with D.C.L. written on it, been let down from
the gallery. The white-headed gentleman blessed
the circumstance. The cap fluttering downwards
paused, either by accident or design, exactly
opposite one of the galleries where a Master of
Arts on duty as Proproctor for the occasion was
standing, and was waved gently within a few
feet of his face. "Put it on, sir!" now came
from all sides of the upper gallery; and somebody
leaning from above the Vice-Chancellor's chair,
seizing the opportunity of a second's lull, said in
a sedate voice, "*Admitto te ad gradum Doctoris*

in jure civili." All this time the intended re-
cipient of this most dubious honour was making
frantic clutches at the cap, which it is needless to
state was bobbed up and down in front of him,
while " Let him have it ! " " He knows what fits
him!" greeted his indignation, which now scarcely
knew bounds. He dashed upstairs to find the
offender ; but, just as his head appeared, the cap
dropped into the area, and his efforts to discover the
author of the offence were fruitless. The entry of
the Vice-Chancellor, followed by the Doctors and
Proctors and various distinguished visitors, and
the pealing of the organ, turned the thoughts of
the undergraduates, and under cover of the music
and applause the irate Proproctor beat an igno-
minious retreat. His conduct was not only un-
popular among the undergraduates, but was con-
demned by senior and junior graduates alike.

The Vice-Chancellor, having taken his seat,
opened Convocation with the usual Latin speech.
Dr. Bryce, Regius Professor of Civil Law, then
presented a number of distinguished men—
bishops, judges, statesmen, soldiers, poets, and
historians—and in introducing each alluded in
brief Latin speeches to the peculiar merits that

had called for the honorary degree of D.C.L.—
the highest honour which the University can
confer. After this the Creweian oration was
delivered by the Public Orator; but as he spoke
in an indistinct voice, and in Latin, the interesting allusions he made to past and present were
scarcely even heard, much less understood. He
took the chaff hurled at him with profound good
humour, and ignoring the various injunctions to
" Speak up," and " That will do, sir—now translate ! " hurried bravely on, and finished amid
cheers of satisfaction. Then came the various
prize poems and essays, to none of which, except
to the Newdigate, was the slightest attention
paid. But the Newdigate, though an exception-
ally good poem, was badly read, and most of the
cheers were ironical—all sorts of absurd construc-
tions being at once fixed upon various lines.

The Masonic Fête on Wednesday afternoon
was very delightful, but they were getting tired
of the incessant gaiety; and so was the Magdalen
concert and Christ-Church ball on Wednesday
night; but they had had enough of concerts and
enough of dancing, and all their energies and
interest were centred in Thursday morning, when

Frank was to take his degree—a far important event to Rose than the conferring of honorary D.C.L. on all the bishops, judges, statesmen, and soldiers put together.

It may be convenient here to enumerate roughly Frank's expenses during his three years' academical career. It will be remembered that his life has been that of an ordinary undergraduate. Its cost is therefore considerably in excess of that of a great many. It is also considerably below the level of comfort and luxury which in some cases folly induces, and in others is justified by adequate means. He came to Oxford not for intellectual advantages only, nor for social advantages only, but for both. He wished to be neither a spendthrift nor a "smug," and he has been neither.

COLLEGE EXPENSES.

(*a*) First outlay.

	£	s.	d.	£	s.	d.
Caution money . .	30	0	0			
Furniture at a valuation .	30	0	0			
Glass, china, &c. . .	9	19	6			
Cap and gown . .	1	2	6			
Books, sundries, and travelling expenses . . .	10	0	0			
	£81	2	0	81	2	0

(b) Terminal.	£	s.	d.	£	s.	d.
Tuition	7	7	0			
Establishment charges .	6	0	0			
Room rent . . .	3	10	0			
Battels, eight weeks, say at						
£2	16	0	0			
Coals, taking term with						
term . . .	2	0	0			
Laundress . . .	1	1	0			
	£35	18	0			
Gratuities to servants .	2	0	0			
	£37	18	$0 \times 9^3 = 341$	2	0	

(c) On taking degree of B.A. . . . 5 0 0

UNIVERSITY FEES.

(a) Matriculation . . .	2	10	0			
(b) Examination Fees.						
Responsions . . .	1	0	0			
Moderations . . .	1	10	0			
Rudiments of Faith and						
Religion . . .	1	0	0			
Honour School of Juris-						
prudence . . .	1	10	0			
(c) On taking degree of B.A. .	7	10	0	15	0	0

<hr>

[3] Three years contain twelve legal terms, but only nine of payment, the Easter and Act terms being virtually one in matter of residence.

Extra Tuition.

	£	s.	d.	£	s.	d.
"Coach" for Moderations	10	10	0			
Reading party to Switzerland . . .	50	0	0			
"Coach" for Jurisprudence, six terms, the College paying half, 60 gs.— 30 gs. . . .	31	10	0	92	0	0

Personal Expenses.

		£	s.	d.
Wines and groceries Clothes and travelling expenses Books and stationery Subscriptions to clubs and societies	} 70 0 0 For three years	210	0	0

Extra Academical.

Inner Temple.	£	s.	d.	£	s.	d.
Entrance form . .	1	1	0			
Stamps . . .	25	1	3			
Fees	10	5	2			
Lecture fees . . .	5	5	0			
	£41	12	5	41	12	5
Annual fees, four terms at	1	6	1	5	4	4

On Thursday morning, having paid to the Dean the necessary College fee, and from him obtained a certificate of twelve terms' residence, Frank, duly attired in cap and gown, white tie, and the statutable garments "of a subfusc hue," proceeded to the Apodyterium of the Convocation House. There he paid the University fee, and showed to the Registrar the testamurs gained in Moderations and the Rudiments of Faith and Religion, and a certificate of his having been placed in the second class in the Honour School of Jurisprudence.

These preliminaries over, he met his party and took them into the Convocation House. There, having waited for half an hour, in a crowd that made moving impossible, and speaking almost a difficulty, the impatient spectators were informed that Convocation was removed to the Sheldonian Theatre, a piece of information certainly welcome, but one which they thought might have been given them before.

Perhaps it need not be said that four hearts at least were filled to overflowing as Frank went up with several other Paul's men to be presented by the Dean to the Vice-Chancellor, and at least one pair of bright eyes shone the brighter for the tears that would rise up in them. And then with

what pride Frank slipped on his gown and tipped
his scout, William, the customary sovereign, and
what a happy party sat down to lunch in Paul's!
Crawford was there, the new Fellow of Queen's,
not yet grown donnish and distant; and little
Blue-eyes too was there, who had made firm
friends with Rose, with whom. she talked with
pride of their two lovers.

In the evening the young people went to Nuneham, Rose and Mary sitting in the stern, Blue-
eyes in the bows, where she paddled in the water
like a very child ; Crawford and Frank rowing.
Mary had brought her sketching-book, and when
they had had tea in the Moss Cottage, and a stroll
was proposed, nothing could induce her to accompany the others. She wanted to sketch the
rustic bridge and the river, and plenty of time
she found for the purpose. For surely never were
folks so long as Rose and Frank, Blue-eyes and
Crawford, in walking through the lovely Nuneham
woods. Like the bright June leaves that hung
over them, life was young, and fresh, and bright ;
sobered, not saddened, by the twilight of earnest
thoughts of the work that lay before them.
Oxford had done her best for these two sons of

hers; had not soured them; had not robbed them of their early faith; had not taught them to posture as the disciples of creeds as meaningless as they are cold and dead; had not inflated them with the notion that Oxford thought leads England and therefore the world; had not elated them with their academical success; but was sending them forth full of energy and full of hope, with the belief that life, that stern hard battle, was beginning and not ending with the winning of a degree.

THE END.

LONDON:
GILBERT AND RIVINGTON, PRINTERS,
ST. JOHN'S SQUARE.

A Catalogue of American and Foreign Books Published or Imported by MESSRS. SAMPSON LOW & CO. *can be had on application.*

Crown Buildings, 188, Fleet Street, London, April, 1879.

𝔄 𝔏𝔦𝔰𝔱 𝔬𝔣 𝔅𝔬𝔬𝔨𝔰

PUBLISHED BY

SAMPSON LOW, MARSTON, SEARLE, & RIVINGTON.

——◆——

ALPHABETICAL LIST.

A CLASSIFIED *Educational Catalogue of Works* published in Great Britain. Demy 8vo, cloth extra. Second Edition, revised and corrected to Christmas, 1877, 5*s.*

Abney (Captain W. de W., R.E., F.R.S.) Thebes, and its Five Greater Temples. Forty large Permanent Photographs, with descriptive letter-press. Super-royal 4to, cloth extra, 63*s.*

About Some Fellows. By an ETON BOY, Author of "A Day of my Life." Cloth limp, square 16mo, 2*s.* 6*d.*

Adventures of Captain Mago. A Phœnician's Explorations 1000 years B.C. By LEON CAHUN. Numerous Illustrations. Crown 8vo, cloth extra, gilt, 7*s.* 6*d.*

Adventures of a Young Naturalist. By LUCIEN BIART, with 117 beautiful Illustrations on Wood. Edited and adapted by PARKER GILLMORE. Post 8vo, cloth extra, gilt edges, New Edition, 7*s.* 6*d.*

Adventures in New Guinea. The Narrative of the Captivity of a French Sailor for Nine Years among the Savages in the Interior. Small post 8vo, with Illustrations and Map, cloth, gilt, 6*s.*

Afghanistan and the Afghans. Being a Brief Review of the History of the Country, and Account of its People. By H. W. BELLEW, C.S.I. Crown 8vo, cloth extra, 6*s.*

Alcott (Louisa M.) Aunt Jo's Scrap-Bag. Square 16mo, 2*s.* 6*d.* (Rose Library, 1*s.*)

—— *Cupid and Chow-Chow.* Small post 8vo, 3*s.* 6*d.*

—— *Little Men: Life at Plumfield with Jo's Boys.* Small post 8vo, cloth, gilt edges, 3*s.* 6*d.* (Rose Library, Double vol. 2*s.*)

—— *Little Women.* 1 vol., cloth, gilt edges, 3*s.* 6*d.* (Rose Library, 2 vols., 1*s.* each.)

—— *Old-Fashioned Girl.* Best Edition, small post 8vo, cloth extra, gilt edges, 3*s.* 6*d.* (Rose Library, 2*s.*)

Alcott (Louisa M.) Work and Beginning Again. A Story of Experience. 1 vol., small post 8vo, cloth extra, 6s. Several Illustrations. (Rose Library, 2 vols., 1s. each.)

—— *Shawl Straps.* Small post 8vo, cloth extra, gilt, 3s. 6d.

—— *Eight Cousins; or, the Aunt Hill.* Small post 8vo, with Illustrations, 3s. 6d.

—— *The Rose in Bloom.* Small post 8vo, cloth extra, 3s. 6d.

—— *Silver Pitchers.* Small post 8vo, cloth extra, 3s. 6d.

—— *Under the Lilacs.* Small post 8vo, cloth extra, 5s.

"Miss Alcott's stories are thoroughly healthy, full of racy fun and humour . . . exceedingly entertaining . . . . We can recommend the 'Eight Cousins.'"— *Athenæum.*

Alpine Ascents and Adventures; or, Rock and Snow Sketches. By H. SCHÜTZ WILSON, of the Alpine Club. With Illustrations by WHYMPER and MARCUS STONE. Crown 8vo, 10s. 6d. 2nd Edition.

Andersen (Hans Christian) Fairy Tales. With Illustrations in Colours by E. V. B. Royal 4to, cloth, 25s.

Andrews (Dr.) Latin-English Lexicon. New Edition. Royal 8vo, 1670 pp., cloth extra, price 18s.

Animals Painted by Themselves. Adapted from the French of Balzac, Georges Sands, &c., with 200 Illustrations by GRANDVILLE. 8vo, cloth extra, gilt, 10s. 6d.

Art of Reading Aloud (The) in Pulpit, Lecture Room, or Private Reunions, with a perfect system of Economy of Lung Power on just principles for acquiring ease in Delivery, and a thorough command of the Voice. By G. VANDENHOFF, M.A. Crown 8vo, cloth extra, 6s.

Asiatic Turkey: being a Narrative of a Journey from Bombay to the Bosphorus, embracing a ride of over One Thousand Miles, from the head of the Persian Gulf to Antioch on the Mediterranean. By GRATTAN GEARY, Editor of the *Times of India.* 2 vols., crown 8vo, cloth extra, with many Illustrations, and a Route Map.

Atlantic Islands as Resorts of Health and Pleasure. By S. G. W. BENJAMIN, Author of "Contemporary Art in Europe," &c. Royal 8vo, cloth extra, with upwards of 150 Illustrations, 16s.

Autobiography of Sir G. Gilbert Scott, R.A., F.S.A., &c. Edited by his Son, G. GILBERT SCOTT. With an Introduction by the DEAN OF CHICHESTER, and a Funeral Sermon, preached in Westminster Abbey, by the DEAN OF WESTMINSTER. Also, Portrait on steel from the portrait of the Author by G. RICHMOND, R.A. 1 vol., demy 8vo, cloth extra, 18s.

BAKER (Lieut.-Gen. Valentine, Pasha). See "War in Bulgaria."

Barton Experiment (The). By the Author of "Helen's Babies." 1s.

THE BAYARD SERIES,

Edited by the late J. HAIN FRISWELL.

Comprising Pleasure Books of Literature produced in the Choicest Style as Companionable Volumes at Home and Abroad.

"We can hardly imagine better books for boys to read or for men to ponder over."—*Times.*

Price 2s. 6d. each Volume, complete in itself, flexible cloth extra, gilt edges, with silk Headbands and Registers.

The Story of the Chevalier Bayard. By M. DE BERVILLE.

De Joinville's St. Louis, King of France.

The Essays of Abraham Cowley, including all his Prose Works.

Abdallah ; or the Four Leaves. By EDOUARD LABOULLAYE.

Table-Talk and Opinions of Napoleon Buonaparte.

Vathek : An Oriental Romance. By WILLIAM BECKFORD.

The King and the Commons. A Selection of Cavalier and Puritan Songs. Edited by Prof. MORLEY.

Words of Wellington: Maxims and Opinions of the Great Duke.

Dr. Johnson's Rasselas, Prince of Abyssinia. With Notes.

Hazlitt's Round Table. With Biographical Introduction.

The Religio Medici, Hydriotaphia, and the Letter to a Friend. By Sir THOMAS BROWNE, Knt.

Ballad Poetry of the Affections. By ROBERT BUCHANAN.

Coleridge's Christabel, and other Imaginative Poems. With Preface by ALGERNON C. SWINBURNE.

Lord Chesterfield's Letters, Sentences, and Maxims. With Introduction by the Editor, and Essay on Chesterfield by M. DE STE.- BEUVE, of the French Academy.

Essays in Mosaic. By THOS. BALLANTYNE.

My Uncle Toby; his Story and his Friends. Edited by P. FITZGERALD.

Reflections; or, Moral Sentences and Maxims of the Duke de la Rochefoucauld.

Socrates : Memoirs for English Readers from Xenophon's Memo- rabilia. By EDW. LEVIEN.

Prince Albert's Golden Precepts.

A Case containing 12 Volumes, price 31s. 6d. ; or the Case separately, price 3s. 6d.

Beauty and the Beast. An Old Tale retold, with Pictures by E. V. B. Demy 4to, cloth extra, novel binding. 10 Illustrations in Colours (in same style as those in the First Edition of "Story without an End "). 12s. 6d.

Benthall (Rev. J.) Songs of the Hebrew Poets in English Verse Crown 8vo, red edges, 10s. 6d.

Beumers' German Copybooks.   In six gradations at 4*d.* each.
Biart (Lucien).   *See* "Adventures of a Young Naturalist,"
  "My Rambles in the New World," "The Two Friends."
Bickersteth's Hymnal Companion to Book of Common Prayer.
  The Original Editions, containing 403 Hymns, always kept in Print.
      Revised and Enlarged Edition, containing 550 Hymns—
⁎⁎ *The Revised Editions are entirely distinct from, and cannot be used with, the*
                        original editions.

				s.	d.
7A	Medium 32mo, cloth limp			0	8
7B	ditto	roan		1	2
7C	ditto	morocco or calf		2	6
8A	Super-royal 32mo, cloth limp			1	0
8B	ditto	red edges		1	2
8C	ditto	roan		2	2
8D	ditto	morocco or calf		3	6
9A	Crown 8vo, cloth, red edges			3	0
9B	ditto	roan		4	0
9C	ditto	morocco or calf		6	0
10A	Crown 8vo, with Introduction and Notes, red edges			4	0
10B	ditto	roan		5	0
10C	ditto	morocco		7	6
11A	Penny Edition in Wrapper			0	1
11B	ditto	cloth		0	2
11G	ditto	fancy cloth		0	4
11C	With Prayer Book, cloth			0	9
11D	ditto	roan		1	0
11E	ditto	morocco		2	6
11F	ditto	persian		1	6
12A	Crown 8vo, with Tunes, cloth, plain edges			4	0
12B	ditto	ditto	persian, red edges	6	6
12C	ditto	ditto	limp morocco, gilt edges	7	6
13A	Small 4to, for Organ			8	6
13B	ditto	ditto	limp russia	21	0
14A	Tonic Sol-fa Edition			3	6
14B	ditto	treble and alto only		1	0
5B	Chants only			1	6
5D	ditto	4to, for Organ		3	6
	The Church Mission Hymn-Book		*per* 100	8	4
	Ditto ditto cloth		*each*	0	4

The "Hymnal Companion" may now be had in special bindings for presentation
with and without the Common Prayer Book. A red line edition is ready.
Lists on application.

Bickersteth (Rev. E. H., M.A.) The Reef and other Parables.
  1 vol., square 8vo, with numerous very beautiful Engravings, 7*s.* 6*d.*
—————— *The Clergyman in his Home.*   Small post 8vo, 1*s.*
—————— *The Master's Home-Call; or, Brief Memorials of*
  Alice Frances Bickersteth. 20th Thousand. 32mo, cloth gilt, 1*s.*
    " They recall in a touching manner a character of which the religious beauty has
  a warmth and grace almost too tender to be definite."—*The Guardian.*

Bickersteth (Rev. E. H., M.A.) The Master's Will. A Funeral Sermon preached on the Death of Mrs. S. Gurney Buxton. Sewn, 6*d.* ; cloth gilt, 1*s.*

———— *The Shadow of the Rock.* A Selection of Religious Poetry. 18mo, cloth extra, 2*s.* 6*d.*

———— *The Shadowed Home and the Light Beyond.* 7th Edition, crown 8vo, cloth extra, 5*s.*

Bida. The Authorized Version of the Four Gospels, with the whole of the magnificent Etchings on Steel, after drawings by M. BIDA, in 4 vols., appropriately bound in cloth extra, price 3*l.* 3*s.* each. Also the four volumes in two, bound in the best morocco, by Suttaby, extra gilt edges, 18*l.* 18*s.*, half-morocco, 12*l.* 12*s.*

"Bida's Illustrations of the Gospels of St. Matthew and St. John have already received here and elsewhere a full recognition of their great merits."—*Times.*

Biographies of the Great Artists, Illustrated. This Series will be issued in Monthly Volumes in the form of Handbooks. Each will be a Monograph of a Great Artist, or a Brief History of a Group of Artists of one School ; and will contain Portraits of the Masters, and as many examples of their art as can be readily procured. They will be Illustrated with from 16 to 20 Full-page Engravings, printed in the best manner, which have been contributed from several of the most important Art-Publications of France and Germany, and will be found valuable records of the Painters' Works. The ornamental binding is taken from an Italian design in a book printed at Venice at the end of the Fifteenth Century, and the inside lining from a pattern of old Italian lace. The price of the Volumes is 3*s.* 6*d.* :—

Titian.	Rubens.	Velasquez.
Rembrandt.	Lionardo.	Tintoret and Veronese.
Raphael.	Turner.	Hogarth.
Van Dyck and Hals.	The Little Masters.	Michelangelo.
Holbein.		

Black (Wm.) Three Feathers. Small post 8vo, cloth extra, 6*s.*

———— *Lady Silverdale's Sweetheart, and other Stories.* 1 vol., small post 8vo. 6*s.*

———— *Kilmeny: a Novel.* Small post 8vo, cloth, 6*s.*

———— *In Silk Attire.* 3rd Edition, small post 8vo, 6*s.*

———— *A Daughter of Heth.* 11th Edition, small post 8vo, 6*s.*

Blackmore (R. D.) Lorna Doone. 10th Edition, cr. 8vo, 6*s.*

"The reader at times holds his breath, so graphically yet so simply does John Ridd tell his tale."—*Saturday Review.*

———— *Alice Lorraine.* 1 vol., small post 8vo, 6th Edition, 6*s*

———— *Clara Vaughan.* Revised Edition, 6*s.*

———— *Cradock Nowell.* New Edition, 6*s.*

———— *Cripps the Carrier.* 3rd Edition, small post 8vo, 6*s.*

Blossoms from the King's Garden : Sermons for Children. By the Rev. C. BOSANQUET. 2nd Edition, small post 8vo, cloth extra, 6s.

Blue Banner (The); or, The Adventures of a Mussulman, a Christian, and a Pagan, in the time of the Crusades and Mongol Conquest. Translated from the French of LEON CAHUN. With Seventy-six Wood Engravings. Square imperial 16mo, cloth extra, 7s. 6d.

Book of English Elegies. By W. F. MARCH PHILLIPPS. Small post 8vo, cloth extra, 5s.
    The Aim of the Editor of this Selection has been to collect in a popular form the best and most representative Elegiac Poems which have been written in the English tongue.

Book of the Play. By DUTTON COOK. 2 vols., crown 8vo, 24s.

Border Tales Round the Camp Fire in the Rocky Mountains. By the Rev. E. B. TUTTLE, Army Chaplain, U.S.A. With Two Illustrations by PHIZ. Crown 8vo, 5s.

Brave Men in Action. By S. J. MACKENNA. Crown 8vo, 480 pp., cloth, 10s. 6d.

Brazil and the Brazilians. By J. C. FLETCHER and D. P. KIDDER. 9th Edition, Illustrated, 8vo, 21s.

Bryant (W. C., assisted by S. H. Gay) A Popular History of the United States. About 4 vols., to be profusely Illustrated with Engravings on Steel and Wood, after Designs by the best Artists. Vol. I., super-royal 8vo, cloth extra, gilt, 42s., is ready.

Burnaby (Capt.) See "On Horseback."

Butler (W. F.) The Great Lone Land; an Account of the Red River Expedition, 1869-70. With Illustrations and Map. Fifth and Cheaper Edition, crown 8vo, cloth extra, 7s. 6d.

—— *The Wild North Land; the Story of a Winter Journey* with Dogs across Northern North America. Demy 8vo, cloth, with numerous Woodcuts and a Map, 4th Edition, 18s. Cr. 8vo, 7s. 6d.

—— *Akim-foo : the History of a Failure.* Demy 8vo, cloth, 2nd Edition, 16s. Also, in crown 8vo, 7s. 6d.

By Land and Ocean ; or, The Journal and Letters of a Tour round the World by a Young Girl *alone*. Crown 8vo, cloth, 7s. 6d.

C*ADOGAN (Lady A.) Illustrated Games of Patience.* Twenty-four Diagrams in Colours, with Descriptive Text. Foolscap 4to, cloth extra, gilt edges, 3rd Edition, 12s. 6d.

Canada under the Administration of Lord Dufferin. By G. STEWART, Jun., Author of "Evenings in the Library," &c. Cloth gilt, 8vo, 15s.

Carbon Process (A Manual of). See LIESEGANG.

Ceramic Art. See JACQUEMART.

Changed Cross (The), and other Religious Poems. 16mo, 2s. 6d.

Chatty Letters from the East and West. By A. H. WYLIE. Small 4to, 12s. 6d.

Child of the Cavern (The) ; or, Strange Doings Underground. By JULES VERNE. Translated by W. H. G. KINGSTON, Author of "Snow Shoes and Canoes," "Peter the Whaler," "The Three Midshipmen," &c., &c., &c. Numerous Illustrations. Square crown 8vo, cloth extra, gilt edges, 7s. 6d.

Child's Play, with 16 Coloured Drawings by E. V. B. Printed on thick paper, with tints, 7s. 6d.

———— *New.* By E. V. B. Similar to the above. *See* New.

Children's Lives and How to Preserve Them ; or, The Nursery Handbook. By W. LOMAS, M.D. Crown 8vo, cloth, 5s.

Choice Editions of Choice Books. 2s. 6d. each, Illustrated by C. W. COPE, R.A., T. CRESWICK, R.A., E. DUNCAN, BIRKET FOSTER, J. C. HORSLEY, A.R.A., G. HICKS, R. REDGRAVE, R.A., C. STONEHOUSE, F. TAYLER, G. THOMAS, H. J. TOWNSHEND, E. H. WEHNERT, HARRISON WEIR, &c.

Bloomfield's Farmer's Boy.	Milton's L'Allegro.
Campbell's Pleasures of Hope.	Poetry of Nature. Harrison Weir.
Coleridge's Ancient Mariner.	Rogers' (Sam.) Pleasures of Memory.
Goldsmith's Deserted Village.	Shakespeare's Songs and Sonnets.
Goldsmith's Vicar of Wakefield.	Tennyson's May Queen.
Gray's Elegy in a Churchyard.	Elizabethan Poets.
Keat's Eve of St. Agnes.	Wordsworth's Pastoral Poems.

" Such works are a glorious beatification for a poet."—*Athenæum.*

Christian Activity. By ELEANOR C. PRICE. Cloth extra, 6s.

Christmas Story-teller (The). By Old Hands and New Ones. Crown 8vo, cloth extra, gilt edges, Fifty-two Illustrations, 10s. 6d.

Church Unity : Thoughts and Suggestions. By the Rev. V. C. KNIGHT, M.A., University College, Oxford. Crown 8vo, pp. 456, 5s.

Clarke (Cowden). See " Recollections of Writers," " Shakespeare Key."

Cobbett (William). A Biography. By EDWARD SMITH. 2 vols., crown 8vo, 25s.

Continental Tour of Eight Days for Forty-four Shillings. By a JOURNEY-MAN. 12mo, 1s.

" The book is simply delightful."—*Spectator.*

Cook (D.) Book of the Play. 2 vols., crown 8vo, 24s.

Copyright, National and International. From the Point of View of a Publisher. Demy 8vo, sewn, 2s.

Covert Side Sketches : Thoughts on Hunting, with Different Packs in Different Countries. By J. NEVITT FITT (H.H. of the *Sporting Gazette,* late of the *Field*). 2nd Edition. Crown 8vo, cloth, 10s. 6d.

Cruise of H.M.S. "Challenger" (The). By W. J. J. SPRY, R.N. With Route Map and many Illustrations. 6th Edition, demy 8vo, cloth, 18s. Cheap Edition, crown 8vo, small type, some of the Illustrations, 7s. 6d.

> "The book before us supplies the information in a manner that leaves little to be desired. 'The Cruise of H.M.S. *Challenger*' is an exceedingly well-written, entertaining, and instructive book."—*United Service Gazette.*
> "Agreeably written, full of information, and copiously illustrated." — *Broad Arrow.*

Curious Adventures of a Field Cricket. By Dr. ERNEST CANDÈZE. Translated by N. D'ANVERS. With numerous fine Illustrations. Crown 8vo, cloth extra, gilt edges, 7s. 6d.

DANA (R. H.) Two Years before the Mast and Twenty-Four years After. Revised Edition with Notes, 12mo, 6s.

Dana (Jas. D.) Corals and Coral Islands. Numerous Illustrations, Charts, &c. New and Cheaper Edition, with numerous important Additions and Corrections. Crown 8vo, cloth extra, 8s. 6d.

Daughter (A) of Heth. By W. BLACK. Crown 8vo, 6s.

Day of My Life (A); or, Every Day Experiences at Eton. By an ETON BOY, Author of "About Some Fellows." 16mo, cloth extra, 2s. 6d. 6th Thousand.

Day out of the Life of a Little Maiden (A): Six Studies from Life. By SHERER and ENGLER. Large 4to, in portfolio, 5s.

Diane. By Mrs. MACQUOID. Crown 8vo, 6s.

Dick Sands, the Boy Captain. By JULES VERNE. With nearly 100 Illustrations, cloth extra, gilt edges, 10s. 6d.

Discoveries of Prince Henry the Navigator, and their Results; being the Narrative of the Discovery by Sea, within One Century, of more than Half the World. By RICHARD HENRY MAJOR, F.S.A. Demy 8vo, with several Woodcuts, 4 Maps, and a Portrait of Prince Henry in Colours. Cloth extra, 15s.

Dodge (Mrs. M.) Hans Brinker; or, the Silver Skates. An entirely New Edition, with 59 Full-page and other Woodcuts. Square crown 8vo, cloth extra, 7s. 6d. ; Text only, paper, 1s.

—— *Theophilus and Others.* 1 vol., small post 8vo, cloth extra, gilt, 3s. 6d.

Dogs of Assize. A Legal Sketch-Book in Black and White. Containing 6 Drawings by WALTER J. ALLEN. Folio, in wrapper, 6s. 8d.

Doré's Spain. See "Spain."

Dougall's (J. D.) Shooting; its Appliances, Practice, and Purpose. With Illustrations, cloth extra, 10s. 6d. See "Shooting."

EARLY History of the Colony of Victoria (The), from its Discovery. By FRANCIS P. LABILLIERE, Fellow of the Royal

Echoes of the Heart. *See* MOODY.

Elinor Dryden. By Mrs. MACQUOID. Crown 8vo, 6s.

English Catalogue of Books (The). Published during 1863 to 1871 inclusive, comprising also important American Publications.
This Volume, occupying over 450 Pages, shows the Titles of 32,000 New Books and New Editions issued during Nine Years, with the Size, Price, and Publisher's Name, the Lists of Learned Societies, Printing Clubs, and other Literary Associations, and the Books issued by them; as also the Publisher's Series and Collections— altogether forming an indispensable adjunct to the Bookseller's Establishment, as well as to every Learned and Literary Club and Association. 30s., half-bound.
*** Of the previous Volume, 1835 to 1862, very few remain on sale; as also of the Index Volume, 1837 to 1857.

—— *Supplements*, 1863, 1864, 1865, 3s. 6d. each; 1866, 1867, to 1879, 5s. each.

Eight Cousins. *See* ALCOTT.

English Writers, Chapters for Self-Improvement in English Literature. By the Author of "The Gentle Life," 6s.

Eton. *See* "Day of my Life," "Out of School," "About Some Fellows."

Evans (C.) Over the Hills and Far Away. By C. EVANS. One Volume, crown 8vo, cloth extra, 10s. 6d.

—— *A Strange Friendship.* Crown 8vo, cloth, 5s.

FAITH Gartney's Girlhood. By the Author of "The Gayworthy's." Fcap. with Coloured Frontispiece, 3s. 6d.

Familiar Letters on some Mysteries of Nature. *See* PHIPSON.

Family Prayers for Working Men. By the Author of "Steps to the Throne of Grace." With an Introduction by the Rev. E. H. BICKERSTETH, M.A., Vicar of Christ Church, Hampstead. Cloth, 1s.

Favell Children (The). Three Little Portraits. Four Illustrations, crown 8vo, cloth gilt, 4s.

Favourite English Pictures. Containing Sixteen Permanent Autotype Reproductions of important Paintings of Modern British Artists. With letterpress descriptions. Atlas 4to, cloth extra, 2l. 2s.

Fern Paradise (The): A Plea for the Culture of Ferns. By F. G. HEATH. New Edition, entirely Rewritten, Illustrated with Eighteen full-page and numerous other Woodcuts, and Four permanent Photographs, large post 8vo, handsomely bound in cloth, 12s. 6d.

Fern World (The). By F. G. HEATH. Illustrated by Twelve Coloured Plates, giving complete Figures (Sixty-four in all) of every Species of British Fern, printed from Nature; by several full-page Engravings; and a permanent Photograph. Large post 8vo, cloth gilt, 400 pp., 4th Edition, 12s. 6d. In 12 parts, sewn, 1s. each.

Few (A) Hints on Proving Wills. Enlarged Edition, 1s.

First Ten Years of a Sailor's Life at Sea. By the Author of
"All About Ships." Demy 8vo, Seventeen full-page Illustrations,
480 pp., 3s. 6d.

Flammarion (C.) The Atmosphere. Translated from the
French of CAMILLE FLAMMARION. Edited by JAMES GLAISHER,
F.R.S. With 10 Chromo-Lithographs and 81 Woodcuts. Royal 8vo,
cloth extra, 30s.

Flooding of the Sahara (The). See MACKENZIE.

Food for the People ; or, Lentils and other Vegetable Cookery.
By E. E. ORLEBAR. Third Thousand. Small post 8vo, boards, 1s.

Footsteps of the Master. See STOWE (Mrs. BEECHER).

Forrest (John) Explorations in Australia. Being Mr. JOHN
FORREST's Personal Account of his Journeys. 1 vol., demy 8vo,
cloth, with several Illustrations and 3 Maps, 16s.

Four Lectures on Electric Induction. Delivered at the Royal
Institution, 1878-9. By J. E. H. GORDON, B.A. Cantab. With
numerous Illustrations. Cloth limp, square 16mo, 3s.

Franc (Maude Jeane). The following form one Series, small
post 8vo, in uniform cloth bindings :—
——— *Emily's Choice.* 5s.
——— *Hall's Vineyard.* 4s.
——— *John's Wife : a Story of Life in South Australia.* 4s.
———- *Marian ; or, the Light of Some One's Home.* 5s.
——— *Silken Cords and Iron Fetters.* 4s.
——— *Vermont Vale.* 5s.
——— *Minnie's Mission.* 4s.
——— *Little Mercy.* 5s.

Funny Foreigners and Eccentric Englishmen. 16 coloured
comic Illustrations for Children. Fcap. folio, coloured wrapper, 4s.

GAMES of Patience. See CADOGAN.

Garvagh (Lord) The Pilgrim of Scandinavia. By LORD
GARVAGH, B.A. Oxford. 8vo, cloth extra, with Illustrations, 10s. 6d.

Geary (Grattan). See " Asiatic Turkey."

Gentle Life (Queen Edition). 2 vols. in 1, small 4to, 10s. 6d.

THE GENTLE LIFE SERIES.

Price 6s. each ; or in calf extra, price 10s. 6d.

The Gentle Life. Essays in aid of the Formation of Character
of Gentlemen and Gentlewomen. 21st Edition.
" Deserves to be printed in letters of gold, and circulated in every house."—
Chambers' Journal.

About in the World. Essays by Author of "The Gentle Life."
" It is not easy to open it at any page without finding some handy idea."—*Morning Post.*

The Gentle Life Series, continued :—

Like unto Christ. A New Translation of Thomas à Kempis' "De Imitatione Christi." With a Vignette from an Original Drawing by Sir THOMAS LAWRENCE. 2nd Edition.

"Could not be presented in a more exquisite form, for a more sightly volume was never seen."—*Illustrated London News.*

Familiar Words. An Index Verborum, or Quotation Handbook. Affording an immediate Reference to Phrases and Sentences that have become embedded in the English language. 3rd and enlarged Edition.

"The most extensive dictionary of quotation we have met with."—*Notes and Queries.*

Essays by Montaigne. Edited and Annotated by the Author of "The Gentle Life." With Portrait. 2nd Edition.

"We should be glad if any words of ours could help to bespeak a large circulation for this handsome attractive book."—*Illustrated Times.*

The Countess of Pembroke's Arcadia. Written by Sir PHILIP SIDNEY. Edited with Notes by Author of "The Gentle Life." 7s. 6d.

"All the best things are retained intact in Mr. Friswell's edition."—*Examiner.*

The Gentle Life. 2nd Series, 8th Edition.

"There is not a single thought in the volume that does not contribute in some measure to the formation of a true gentleman."—*Daily News.*

Varia : Readings from Rare Books. Reprinted, by permission, from the *Saturday Review, Spectator,* &c.

"The books discussed in this volume are no less valuable than they are rare, and the compiler is entitled to the gratitude of the public."—*Observer.*

The Silent Hour: Essays, Original and Selected. By the Author of "The Gentle Life." 3rd Edition.

"All who possess 'The Gentle Life' should own this volume."—*Standard.*

Half-Length Portraits. Short Studies of Notable Persons. By J. HAIN FRISWELL. Small post 8vo, cloth extra, 6s.

Essays on English Writers, for the Self-improvement of Students in English Literature.

"To all who have neglected to read and study their native literature we would certainly suggest the volume before us as a fitting introduction."—*Examiner.*

Other People's Windows. By J. HAIN FRISWELL. 3rd Edition.

"The chapters are so lively in themselves, so mingled with shrewd views of human nature, so full of illustrative anecdotes, that the reader cannot fail to be amused."—*Morning Post.*

A Man's Thoughts. By J. HAIN FRISWELL.

German Primer. Being an Introduction to First Steps in German. By M. T. PREU. 2s. 6d.

Getting On in the World ; or, Hints on Success in Life. By W. MATHEWS, LL.D. Small post 8vo, cloth, 2s. 6d.; gilt edges, 3s. 6d.

Gilliatt (Rev. E.) On the Wolds. 2 vols., crown 8vo, 21s.

Gilpin's Forest Scenery. Edited by F. G. HEATH. 1 vol., large post 8vo, with numerous Illustrations. Uniform with "The Fern World" and "Our Woodland Trees." 12*s.* 6*d.*

Gordon (J. E. H.). See "Four Lectures on Electric Induction," "Practical Treatise on Electricity," &c.

Gouffé. The Royal Cookery Book. By JULES GOUFFÉ; translated and adapted for English use by ALPHONSE GOUFFÉ, Head Pastrycook to her Majesty the Queen. Illustrated with large plates printed in colours. 161 Woodcuts, 8vo, cloth extra, gilt edges, 2*l.* 2*s.*

—— Domestic Edition, half-bound, 10*s.* 6*d.*

"By far the ablest and most complete work on cookery that has ever been submitted to the gastronomical world."—*Pall Mall Gazette.*

—— *The Book of Preserves ; or, Receipts for Preparing and* Preserving Meat, Fish salt and smoked, &c., &c. 1 vol., royal 8vo, containing upwards of 500 Receipts and 34 Illustrations, 10*s.* 6*d.*

—— *Royal Book of Pastry and Confectionery.* By JULES GOUFFÉ, Chef-de-Cuisine of the Paris Jockey Club. Royal 8vo, Illustrated with 10 Chromo-lithographs and 137 Woodcuts, from Drawings by E. MONJAT. Cloth extra, gilt edges, 35*s.*

Gouraud (Mdlle.) Four Gold Pieces. Numerous Illustrations. Small post 8vo, cloth, 2*s.* 6*d. See also* Rose Library.

Government of M. Thiers. By JULES SIMON. Translated from the French. 2 vols., demy 8vo, cloth extra, 32*s.*

Gower (Lord Ronald) Handbook to the Art Galleries, Public and Private, of Belgium and Holland. 18mo, cloth, 5*s.*

—— *The Castle Howard Portraits.* 2 vols., folio, cl. extra, 6*l.* 6*s.*

Greek Grammar. See WALLER.

Guizot's History of France. Translated by ROBERT BLACK. Super-royal 8vo, very numerous Full-page and other Illustrations. In 5 vols., cloth extra, gilt, each 24*s.*

"It supplies a want which has long been felt, and ought to be in the hands of all students of history."—*Times.*

"Three-fourths of M. Guizot's great work are now completed, and the 'History of France,' which was so nobly planned, has been hitherto no less admirably executed."—*From long Review of Vol. III. in the Times.*

"M. Guizot's main merit is this, that, in a style at once clear and vigorous, he sketches the essential and most characteristic features of the times and personages described, and seizes upon every salient point which can best illustrate and bring out to view what is most significant and instructive in the spirit of the age described."—*Evening Standard,* Sept. 23, 1874.

—— *History of England.* In 3 vols. of about 500 pp. each, containing 60 to 70 Full-page and other Illustrations, cloth extra, gilt, 24*s.* each.

"For luxury of typography, plainness of print, and beauty of illustration, these volumes, of which but one has as yet appeared in English, will hold their own against any production of an age so luxurious as our own in everything, typography not excepted."—*Times.*

Guillemin. See "World of Comets."

Guyon (Mde.) Life. By UPHAM. 6th Edition, crown 8vo, 6*s.*

Guyot (*A.*) *Physical Geography.* By ARNOLD GUYOT, Author of "Earth and Man." In 1 volume, large 4to, 128 pp., numerous coloured Diagrams, Maps, and Woodcuts, price 10s. 6d.

HABITATIONS of Man in all Ages. See LE-DUC.

Hamilton (*A. H. A., J.P.*) See "Quarter Sessions."
Handbook to the Charities of London. See LOW's.
———————— *Principal Schools of England.* See Practical.
Half-Hours of Blind Man's Holiday ; or, Summer and Winter Sketches in Black & White. By W. W. FENN. 2 vols., cr. 8vo, 24s.
Half-Length Portraits. Short Studies of Notable Persons. By J. HAIN FRISWELL. Small post 8vo, cloth extra, 6s.
Hall (*W. W.*) *How to Live Long; or,* 1408 *Health Maxims,* Physical, Mental, and Moral. By W. W. HALL, A.M., M.D. Small post 8vo, cloth, 2s. Second Edition.
Hans Brinker; or, the Silver Skates. See DODGE.
Heart of Africa. Three Years' Travels and Adventures in the Unexplored Regions of Central Africa, from 1868 to 1871. By Dr. GEORG SCHWEINFURTH. Translated by ELLEN E. FREWER. With an Introduction by WINWOOD READE. An entirely New Edition, revised and condensed by the Author. Numerous Illustrations, and large Map. 2 vols., crown 8vo, cloth, 15s.
Heath (*F. G.*). See "Fern World," "Fern Paradise," "Our Woodland Trees," "Trees and Ferns."
Heber's (*Bishop*) *Illustrated Edition of Hymns.* With upwards of 100 beautiful Engravings. Small 4to, handsomely bound, 7s. 6d. Morocco, 18s. 6d. and 21s. An entirely New Edition.
Hector Servadac. See VERNE. The heroes of this story were carried away through space on the Comet "Gallia," and their adventures are recorded with all Jules Verne's characteristic spirit. With nearly 100 Illustrations, cloth extra, gilt edges, 10s. 6d.
Henderson (*A.*) *Latin Proverbs and Quotations ;* with Translations and Parallel Passages, and a copious English Index. By ALFRED HENDERSON. Fcap. 4to, 530 pp., 10s. 6d.
History and Handbook of Photography. Translated from the French of GASTON TISSANDIER. Edited by J. THOMSON. Imperial 16mo, over 300 pages, 70 Woodcuts, and Specimens of Prints by the best Permanent Processes. Second Edition, with an Appendix by the late Mr. HENRY FOX TALBOT, giving an account of his researches. Cloth extra, 6s.
History of a Crime (*The*) *; Deposition of an Eye-witness.* By VICTOR HUGO. 4 vols., crown 8vo, 42s. Cheap Edition, 1 vol., 6s.
———— *England.* See GUIZOT.
———— *France.* See GUIZOT.
———— *Russia.* See RAMBAUD.

History of Merchant Shipping. See LINDSAY.

———— *United States.* See BRYANT.

———— *Ireland.* By STANDISH O'GRADY. Vol. I. ready, 7s. 6d.

———— *American Literature.* By M. C. TYLER. Vols. I. and II., 2 vols, 8vo, 24s.

History and Principles of Weaving by Hand and by Power. With several hundred Illustrations. By ALFRED BARLOW. Royal 8vo, cloth extra, 1l. 5s.

Hitherto. By the Author of " The Gayworthys." New Edition, cloth extra, 3s. 6d. Also, in Rose Library, 2 vols., 2s.

Hofmann (Carl). A Practical Treatise on the Manufacture of Paper in all its Branches. Illustrated by 110 Wood Engravings, and 5 large Folding Plates. In 1 vol., 4to, cloth ; about 400 pp., 3l. 13s. 6d.

Home of the Eddas. By C. G. LOCK. Demy 8vo, cloth, 16s.

How to Build a House. See LE-DUC.

How to Live Long. See HALL.

Hugo (Victor) "Ninety-Three." Illustrated. Crown 8vo, 6s.

———— *Toilers of the Sea.* Crown 8vo. Illustrated, 6s. ; fancy boards, 2s. ; cloth, 2s. 6d. ; On large paper with all the original Illustrations, 10s. 6d.

———— *See* "History of a Crime."

Hundred Greatest Men (The). Eight vols., 21s. each. See below.

> "Messrs. SAMPSON LOW & Co. are about to issue an important 'International' work, entitled, 'THE HUNDRED GREATEST MEN :' being the Lives and Portraits of the 100 Greatest Men of History, divided into Eight Classes, each Class to form a Monthly Quarto Volume. The Introductions to the volumes are to be written by recognized authorities on the different subjects, the English contributors being DEAN STANLEY, Mr. MATTHEW ARNOLD. Mr. FROUDE, and Professor MAX MÜLLER: in Germany, Professor HELMHOLTZ; in France, MM. TAINE and RENAN ; and in America, Mr. EMERSON. The Portraits are to be Reproductions from fine and rare Steel Engravings."—*Academy.*

Hunting, Shooting, and Fishing ; A Sporting Miscellany. Illustrated. Crown 8vo, cloth extra, 7s. 6d.

Hymnal Companion to Book of Common Prayer. See BICKERSTETH.

ILLUSTRATIONS of China and its People. By J. THOMSON, F.R.G.S. Four Volumes, imperial 4to, each 3l. 3s.

In my Indian Garden. By PHIL. ROBINSON. With a Preface by EDWIN ARNOLD, M.A., C.S.I., &c. Crown 8vo, limp cloth, 3s. 6d.

Irish Bar. Comprising Anecdotes, Bon-Mots, and Bio-graphical Sketches of the Bench and Bar of Ireland. By J. RODERICK O'FLANAGAN, Barrister-at-Law. Crown 8vo, 12s. Second Edition.

JACQUEMART (A.) History of the Ceramic Art: De-scriptive and Analytical Study of the Potteries of all Times and of

Catenacci and J. Jacquemart. 12 Steel-plate Engravings, and 1000 Marks and Monograms. Translated by Mrs. BURY PALLISER. In 1 vol., super-royal 8vo, of about 700 pp., cloth extra, gilt edges, 28s.

"This is one of those few gift-books which, while they can certainly lie on a table and look beautiful, can also be read through with real pleasure and profit."—*Times.*

*K*ENNEDY'S *(Capt. W. R.) Sporting Adventures in the* Pacific. With Illustrations, demy 8vo, 18s.

—— *(Capt. A. W. M. Clark).* See "To the Arctic Regions."

Khedive's Egypt (The); or, The old House of Bondage under New Masters. By EDWIN DE LEON. Illustrated. Demy 8vo, cloth extra, Third Edition, 18s. Cheap Edition, 8s. 6d.

Kingston (W. H. G.). See "Snow-Shoes."

—— *Child of the Cavern.*

—— *Two Supercargoes.*

—— *With Axe and Rifle.*

Koldewey (Capt.) The Second North German Polar Expedition in the Year 1869-70. Edited and condensed by H. W. BATES. Numerous Woodcuts, Maps, and Chromo-lithographs. Royal 8vo, cloth extra, 1l. 15s.

*L*ADY *Silverdale's Sweetheart. 6s. See* BLACK.

Land of Bolivar (The); or, War, Peace, and Adventure in the Republic of Venezuela. By JAMES MUDIE SPENCE, F.R.G.S., F.Z.S. 2 vols., demy 8vo, cloth extra, with numerous Woodcuts and Maps, 31s. 6d. Second Edition.

Landseer Gallery (The). Containing thirty-six Autotype Reproductions of Engravings from the most important early works of Sir EDWIN LANDSEER. With a Memoir of the Artist's Life, and Descriptions of the Plates. Imperial 4to, cloth, gilt edges, 2l. 2s.

Le-Duc (V.) How to build a House. By VIOLLET-LE-DUC, Author of "The Dictionary of Architecture," &c. Numerous Illustrations, Plans, &c. Medium 8vo, cloth, gilt, 12s.

—— *Annals of a Fortress.* Numerous Illustrations and Diagrams. Demy 8vo, cloth extra, 15s.

—— *The Habitations of Man in all Ages.* By E. VIOLLET-LE-DUC. Illustrated by 103 Woodcuts. Translated by BENJAMIN BUCKNALL, Architect. 8vo, cloth extra, 16s.

—— *Lectures on Architecture.* By VIOLLET-LE-DUC. Translated from the French by BENJAMIN BUCKNALL, Architect. In 2 vols., royal 8vo, 3l. 3s. Also in Parts, 10s. 6d. each.

—— *Mont Blanc: a Treatise on its Geodesical and Geo*logical Constitution—its Transformations, and the Old and Modern state of its Glaciers. By EUGENE VIOLLET-LE-DUC. With 120 Illustrations. Translated by B. BUCKNALL. 1 vol., demy 8vo, 14s.

Le-Duc (V.) On Restoration; with a Notice of his Works by CHARLES WETHERED. Crown 8vo, with a Portrait on Steel of VIOLLET-LE-DUC, cloth extra, 2s. 6d.

Lenten Meditations. In Two Series, each complete in itself. By the Rev. CLAUDE BOSANQUET, Author of "Blossoms from the King's Garden." 16mo, cloth, First Series, 1s. 6d.; Second Series, 2s.

Lentils. See "Food for the People."

Liesegang (Dr. Paul E.) A Manual of the Carbon Process of Photography. Demy 8vo, half-bound, with Illustrations, 4s.

Life and Letters of the Honourable Charles Sumner (The). 2 vols., royal 8vo, cloth. The Letters give full description of London Society—Lawyers—Judges—Visits to Lords Fitzwilliam, Leicester, Wharncliffe, Brougham—Association with Sydney Smith, Hallam, Macaulay, Dean Milman, Rogers, and Talfourd; also, a full Journal which Sumner kept in Paris. Second Edition, 36s.

Lindsay (W. S.) History of Merchant Shipping and Ancient Commerce. Over 150 Illustrations, Maps and Charts. In 4 vols., demy 8vo, cloth extra. Vols. 1 and 2, 21s.; vols. 3 and 4, 24s. each.

Lion Jack : a Story of Perilous Adventures amongst Wild Men and Beasts. Showing how Menageries are made. By P. T. BARNUM. With Illustrations. Crown 8vo, cloth extra, price 6s.

Little King; or, the Taming of a Young Russian Count. By S. BLANDY. Translated from the French. 64 Illustrations. Crown 8vo, cloth extra, gilt, 7s. 6d.

Little Mercy; or, For Better for Worse. By MAUDE JEANNE FRANC, Author of "Marian," "Vermont Vale," &c., &c. Small post 8vo, cloth extra, 4s.

Long (Col. C. Chaillé) Central Africa. Naked Truths of Naked People : an Account of Expeditions to Lake Victoria Nyanza and the Mabraka Niam-Niam. Demy 8vo, numerous Illustrations, 18s.

Lord Collingwood : a Biographical Study. By. W. DAVIS. With Steel Engraving of Lord Collingwood. Crown 8vo, 2s.

Lost Sir Massingberd. New Edition, 16mo, boards, coloured wrapper, 2s.

Low's German Series—

1. **The Illustrated German Primer.** Being the easiest introduction to the study of German for all beginners. 1s.
2. **The Children's own German Book.** A Selection of Amusing and Instructive Stories in Prose. Edited by Dr. A. L. MEISSNER, Professor of Modern Languages in the Queen's University in Ireland. Small post 8vo, cloth, 1s. 6d.
3. **The First German Reader, for Children from Ten to** Fourteen. Edited by Dr. A. L. MEISSNER. Small post 8vo, cloth, 1s. 6d.
4. **The Second German Reader.** Edited by Dr. A. L. MEISSNER, Small post 8vo, cloth, 1s. 6d.

Low's German Series, continued :—

Buchheim's Deutsche Prosa.   Two Volumes, sold separately :—

5. **Schiller's Prosa.** Containing Selections from the Prose Works of Schiller, with Notes for English Students. By Dr. BUCHHEIM, Professor of the German Language and Literature, King's College, London. Small post 8vo, 2*s.* 6*d.*

6. **Goethe's Prosa.** Containing Selections from the Prose Works of Goethe, with Notes for English Students. By Dr. BUCHHEIM. Small post 8vo, 3*s.* 6*d.*

Low's Standard Library of Travel and Adventure. Crown 8vo, bound uniformly in cloth extra, price 7*s.* 6*d.*

1. **The Great Lone Land.** By W. F. BUTLER, C.B.
2. **The Wild North Land.** By W. F. BUTLER, C.B.
3. **How I found Livingstone.** By H. M. STANLEY.
4. **The Threshold of the Unknown Region.** By C. R. MARKHAM. (4th Edition, with Additional Chapters, 10*s.* 6*d.*)
5. **A Whaling Cruise to Baffin's Bay and the Gulf of Boothia.** By A. H. MARKHAM.
6. **Campaigning on the Oxus.** By J. A. MACGAHAN.
7. **Akim-foo: the History of a Failure.** By MAJOR W. F. BUTLER, C.B.
8. **Ocean to Ocean.** By the Rev. GEORGE M. GRANT. With Illustrations.
9. **Cruise of the Challenger.** By W. J. J. SPRY, R.N.
10. **Schweinfurth's Heart of Africa.** 2 vols., 15*s.*

Low's Standard Novels. Crown 8vo, 6*s.* each, cloth extra.

Three Feathers. By WILLIAM BLACK.
A Daughter of Heth. 13th Edition.   By W. BLACK.   With Frontispiece by F. WALKER, A.R.A.
Kilmeny. A Novel. By W. BLACK.
In Silk Attire. By W. BLACK.
Lady Silverdale's Sweetheart. By W. BLACK.
Alice Lorraine. By R. D. BLACKMORE.
Lorna Doone. By R. D. BLACKMORE. 8th Edition.
Cradock Nowell. By R. D. BLACKMORE.
Clara Vaughan. By R. D. BLACKMORE.
Cripps the Carrier. By R. D. BLACKMORE.
Innocent. By Mrs. OLIPHANT.   Eight Illustrations.
Work. A Story of Experience. By LOUISA M. ALCOTT.   Illustrations.   *See also* Rose Library.
A French Heiress in her own Chateau. By the author of "One Only," "Constantia," &c.   Six Illustrations.
Ninety-Three. By VICTOR HUGO.   Numerous Illustrations.
My Wife and I. By Mrs. BEECHER STOWE.
Wreck of the Grosvenor. By W. CLARK RUSSELL.
Elinor Dryden. By Mrs. MACQUOID.
Diane. By Mrs. MACQUOID.

Low's Handbook to the Charities of London for 1879. Edited
and revised to July, 1879, by C. MACKESON, F.S.S., Editor of
"A Guide to the Churches of London and its Suburbs," &c. 1*s.*

MACGAHAN (J. A.) Campaigning on the Oxus, and the
Fall of Khiva. With Map and numerous Illustrations, 4th Edition,
small post 8vo, cloth extra, 7*s.* 6*d.*

———— *Under the Northern Lights; or, the Cruise of the*
"Pandora" to Peel's Straits, in Search of Sir John Franklin's Papers.
With Illustrations by Mr. DE WYLDE, who accompanied the Expedi-
tion. Demy 8vo, cloth extra, 18*s.*

Macgregor (John) "Rob Roy" on the Baltic. 3rd Edition
small post 8vo, 2*s.* 6*d.*

———— *A Thousand Miles in the "Rob Roy" Canoe.* 11th
Edition, small post 8vo, 2*s.* 6*d.*

———— *Description of the "Rob Roy" Canoe,* with Plans, &c., 1*s.*

———— *The Voyage Alone in the Yawl "Rob Roy."* New
Edition, thoroughly revised, with additions, small post 8vo, 5*s.*

Mackenzie (D). The Flooding of the Sahara. An Account of
the Project for opening direct communication with 38,000,000 people.
With a Description of North-West Africa and Soudan. By DONALD
MACKENZIE. 8vo, cloth extra, with Illustrations, 10*s.* 6*d.*

Macquoid (Mrs.) Elinor Dryden. Crown 8vo, cloth, 6*s.*

———— *Diane.* Crown 8vo, 6*s.*

Marked Life (A); or, The Autobiography of a Clairvoyante.
By "GIPSY." Post 8vo, 5*s.*

Markham (A. H.) The Cruise of the "Rosario." By A. H.
MARKHAM, R.N. 8vo, cloth extra, with Map and Illustrations.

———— *A Whaling Cruise to Baffin's Bay and the Gulf of*
Boothia. With an Account of the Rescue by his Ship, of the Survivors of the Crew of the "Polaris;" and a Description of Modern
Whale Fishing. 3rd and Cheaper Edition, crown 8vo, 2 Maps and
several Illustrations, cloth extra, 7*s.* 6*d.*

Markham (C. R.) The Threshold of the Unknown Region.
Crown 8vo, with Four Maps, 4th Edition, with Additional Chapters,
giving the History of our present Expedition, as far as known, and an
Account of the Cruise of the "Pandora." Cloth extra, 10*s.* 6*d.*

Maury (Commander) Physical Geography of the Sea, and its
Meteorology. Being a Reconstruction and Enlargement of his former
Work, with Charts and Diagrams. New Edition, crown 8vo, 6*s.*

Men of Mark: a Gallery of Contemporary Portraits of the most
Eminent Men of the Day taken from Life, especially for this publica-
tion, price 1*s.* 6*d.* monthly. Vols. I., II., and III. handsomely bound,
cloth, gilt edges, 25*s.* each.

Mercy Philbrick's Choice. Small post 8vo, 3*s.* 6*d.*
"The story is of a high character, and the play of feeling is very subtilely and
cleverly wrought out."—*British Quarterly Review.*

Michael Strogoff. 10s. 6d. *See* VERNE.

Michie (Sir A., K.C.M.G.) See "Readings in Melbourne."

Mitford (Miss). See "Our Village."

Mohr (E.) To the Victoria Falls of the Zambesi. By EDWARD MOHR. Translated by N. D'ANVÉRS. Numerous Full-page and other Woodcut Illustrations, Four Chromo-lithographs, and Map. Demy 8vo, cloth extra, 24s.

Montaigne's Essays. See "Gentle Life Series."

Mont Blanc. See LE-DUC.

Moody (Emma) Echoes of the Heart. A Collection of upwards of 200 Sacred Poems. 16mo, cloth, gilt edges, 3s. 6d.

My Brother Jack; or, The Story of Whatd'yecallem. Written by Himself. From the French of ALPHONSE DAUDET. Illustrated by P. PHILIPPOTEAUX. Square imperial 16mo, cloth extra, 7s. 6d.
      " He would answer to Hi ! or to any loud cry,
      To What-you-may-call-'em, or What was his name ;
      But especially Thingamy-jig."—*Hunting of the Snark.*

My Rambles in the New World. By LUCIEN BIART, Author of "The Adventures of a Young Naturalist." Crown 8vo, cloth extra. Numerous full-page Illustrations, 7s. 6d.

Mysterious Island. By JULES VERNE. 3 vols., imperial 16mo. 150 Illustrations, cloth gilt, 3s. 6d. each ; elaborately bound, gilt edges, 7s. 6d. each.

NARES (Sir G. S., K.C.B.) Narrative of a Voyage to the Polar Sea during 1875-76, in H.M.'s Ships "Alert" and "Discovery." By Captain Sir G. S. NARES, R.N., K.C.B., F.R.S. Published by permission of the Lords Commissioners of the Admiralty. With Notes on the Natural History, edited by H. W. FEILDEN, F.G.S., C.M.Z.S., F.R.G.S., Naturalist to the Expedition. Two Volumes, demy 8vo, with numerous Woodcut Illustrations, Photographs, &c. 4th Edition, 2l. 2s.

New Child's Play (A). Sixteen Drawings by E. V. B. Beautifully printed in colours, 4to, cloth extra, 12s. 6d.

New Ireland. By A. M. SULLIVAN, M.P. for Louth. 2 vols., demy 8vo, cloth extra, 30s. One of the main objects which the Author has had in view in writing this work has been to lay before England and the world a faithful history of Ireland, in a series of descriptive sketches of the episodes in Ireland's career during the last quarter of a century. Cheaper Edition, 1 vol., crown 8vo, 8s. 6d.

New Testament. The Authorized English Version ; with various readings from the most celebrated Manuscripts. Cloth flexible, gilt edges, 2s. 6d. ; cheaper style, 2s. ; or sewed, 1s. 6d.

Noble Words and Noble Deeds. Translated from the French of E. MULLER, by DORA LEIGH. Containing many Full-page Illustrations by PHILIPPOTEAUX. Square imperial 16mo, cloth extra, 7s. 6d.
      "This is a book which will delight the young. . . . We cannot imagine a nicer present than this book for children."—*Standard.*
      " Is certain to become a favourite with young people."—*Court Journal.*

North American Review (*The*).　Monthly, price 2*s.* 6*d.*

Notes and Sketches of an Architect taken during a Journey in the North-West of Europe.　Translated from the French of FELIX NAR-JOUX. 214 Full-page and other Illustrations. Demy 8vo, cloth extra, 16*s.*
　"His book is vivacious and sometimes brilliant. It is admirably printed and illustrated."—*British Quarterly Review.*

Notes on Fish and Fishing.　By the Rev. J. J. MANLEY, M.A. With Illustrations, crown 8vo, cloth extra, leatherette binding, 10*s.* 6*d.*
　"We commend the work."—*Field.*
　"He has a page for every day in the year, or nearly so, and there is not a dull one amongst them."—*Notes and Queries.*
　"A pleasant and attractive volume."—*Graphic.*
　"Brightly and pleasantly written."—*John Bull.*

Novels.　Crown 8vo, cloth, 10*s.* 6*d.* per vol. :—

Mary Anerley. By R. D. BLACKMORE, Author of "Lorna Doone," &c.　3 vols.　　　　　　　　　　　　　　[*In the press.*

An Old Story of My Farming Days. By FRITZ REUTER, Author of "In the Year '13."　3 vols.

All the World's a Stage. By M. A. M. HOPPUS, Author of "Five Chimnney Farm."　3 vols.

Cressida. By M. B. THOMAS.　3 vols.

Elizabeth Eden.　3 vols.

The Martyr of Glencree. A Story of the Persecutions in Scotland in the Reign of Charles the Second. By R. SOMERS.　3 vols.

The Cat and Battledore, and other Stories, translated from Balzac.　3 vols.

A Woman of Mind.　3 vols.

The Cossacks. By COUNT TOLSTOY. Translated from the Russian by EUGENE SCHUYLER, Author of "Turkistan."　2 vols.

The Hour will Come: a Tale of an Alpine Cloister. By WILHEL-MINE VON HILLERN, Author of "The Vulture Maiden." Trans-lated from the German by CLARA BELL.　2 vols.

A Stroke of an Afghan Knife. By R. A. STERNDALE, F.R.G.S., Author of "Seonee."　3 vols.

The Braes of Yarrow. By C. GIBBON.　3 vols.

Auld Lang Syne. By the Author of "The Wreck of the Grosvenor." 2 vols.

Written on their Foreheads. By R. H. ELLIOT.　2 vols.

On the Wolds. By the Rev. E. GILLIAT, Author of "Asylum Christi."　2 vols.

In a Rash Moment. By JESSIE MCLAREN.　2 vols.

Old Charlton. By BADEN PRITCHARD.　3 vols.
　"Mr. Baden Pritchard has produced a well-written and interesting story."—*Scotsman.*

Nursery Playmates (*Prince of*).　217 Coloured pictures for Children by eminent Artists.　Folio, in coloured boards, 6*s.*

*O*CEAN *to Ocean : Sandford Fleming's Expedition through* Canada in 1872.　By the Rev. GEORGE M. GRANT. With Illustra-tions. Revised and enlarged Edition, crown 8vo, cloth, 7*s.* 6*d.*

Old-Fashioned Girl. See ALCOTT.

Oleographs. (Catalogues and price lists on application.)

Oliphant (Mrs.) Innocent. A Tale of Modern Life. By Mrs. OLIPHANT, Author of "The Chronicles of Carlingford," &c., &c. With Eight Full-page Illustrations, small post 8vo, cloth extra, 6s.

On Horseback through Asia Minor. By Capt. FRED BURNABY, Royal Horse Guards, Author of "A Ride to Khiva." 2 vols., 8vo, with three Maps and Portrait of Author, 6th Edition, 38s. This work describes a ride of over 2000 miles through the heart of Asia Minor, and gives an account of five months with Turks, Circassians, Christians, and Devil-worshippers. Cheaper Edition, crown 8vo, 10s. 6d.

On Restoration. See LE-DUC.

On Trek in the Transvaal ; or, Over Berg and Veldt in South Africa. By H. A. ROCHE. Crown 8vo, cloth, 10s. 6d. 4th Edition.

Orlebar (Eleanor E.) See "Sancta Christina," "Food for the People."

Our Little Ones in Heaven. Edited by the Rev. H. ROBBINS. With Frontispiece after Sir JOSHUA REYNOLDS. Fcap., cloth extra, New Edition—the 3rd, with Illustrations, 5s.

Our Village. By MARY RUSSELL MITFORD. Illustrated with Frontispiece Steel Engraving, and 12 full-page and 157 smaller Cuts of Figure Subjects and Scenes, from Drawings by W. H. J. BOOT and C. O. MURRAY. Chiefly from Sketches made by these Artists in the neighbourhood of "Our Village." Crown 4to, cloth extra, gilt edges, 21s.

Our Woodland Trees. By F. G. HEATH. Large post 8vo, cloth, gilt edges, uniform with "Fern World" and "Fern Paradise," by the same Author. 8 Coloured Plates and 20 Woodcuts, 12s. 6d.

Out of School at Eton. Being a collection of Poetry and Prose Writings. By SOME PRESENT ETONIANS. Foolscap 8vo, cloth, 3s. 6d.

PAINTERS of All Schools. By LOUIS VIARDOT, and other Writers. 500 pp., super-royal 8vo, 20 Full-page and 70 smaller Engravings, cloth extra, 25s. A New Edition is being issued in Half-crown parts, with fifty additional portraits, cloth, gilt edges, 31s. 6d.

"A handsome volume, full of information and sound criticism."—*Times.*
"Almost an encyclopædia of painting. . . . . It may be recommended as a handy and elegant guide to beginners in the study of the history of art."—*Saturday Review.*

Palliser (Mrs.) A History of Lace, from the Earliest Period. A New and Revised Edition, with additional cuts and text, upwards of 100 Illustrations and coloured Designs. 1 vol. 8vo, 1l. 1s.

"One of the most readable books of the season ; permanently valuable, always interesting, often amusing, and not inferior in all the essentials of a gift book."—*Times.*

—— *Historic Devices, Badges, and War Cries.* 8vo, 1l. 1s.

Palliser (Mrs.) The China Collector's Pocket Companion. With upwards of 1000 Illustrations of Marks and Monograms. 2nd Edition, with Additions. Small post 8vo, limp cloth, 5s.

"We scarcely need add that a more trustworthy and convenient handbook does not exist, and that others besides ourselves will feel grateful to Mrs. Palliser for the care and skill she has bestowed upon it."—*Academy.*

Petites Leçons de Conversation et de Grammaire: Oral and Conversational Method ; being Little Lessons introducing the most Useful Topics of Daily Conversation, upon an entirely new principle, &c. By F. JULIEN, French Master at King Edward the Sixth's Grammar School, Birmingham. Author of "The Student's French Examiner," which see.

Phillips (L.) Dictionary of Biographical Reference. 8vo, 1l. 11s. 6d.

Phipson (Dr. T. L.) Familiar Letters on some Mysteries of Nature and Discoveries in Science. Crown 8vo, cloth extra, 7s. 6d.

Photography (History and Handbook of). See TISSANDIER.

Picture Gallery of British Art (The). 38 Permanent Photographs after the most celebrated English Painters. With Descriptive Letterpress. Vols. 1 to 5, cloth extra, 18s. each. Vol. 6 for 1877, commencing New Series, demy folio, 31s. 6d. Monthly Parts, 1s. 6d.

Pike (N.) Sub-Tropical Rambles in the Land of the Aphanapteryx. In 1 vol., demy 8vo, 18s. Profusely Illustrated from the Author's own Sketches. Also with Maps and Meteorological Charts.

Placita Anglo-Normannica. The Procedure and Constitution of the Anglo-Norman Courts (WILLIAM I.—RICHARD I.), as shown by Contemporaneous Records ; all the Reports of the Litigation of the period, as recorded in the Chronicles and Histories of the time, being gleaned and literally transcribed. With Explanatory Notes, &c. By M. M. BIGELOW. Demy 8vo, cloth, 21s.

Plutarch's Lives. An Entirely New and Library Edition. Edited by A. H. CLOUGH, Esq. 5 vols., 8vo, 2l. 10s.; half-morocco, gilt top, 3l. Also in 1 vol., royal 8vo, 800 pp., cloth extra, 18s.; half-bound, 21s.

—— *Morals.* Uniform with Clough's Edition of "Lives of Plutarch." Edited by Professor GOODWIN. 5 vols., 8vo, 3l. 3s.

Poe (E. A.) The Works of. 4 vols., 2l. 2s.

Poems of the Inner Life. A New Edition, Revised, with many additional Poems, inserted by permission of the Authors. Small post 8vo, cloth, 5s.

Poganuc People: their Loves and Lives. By Mrs. BEECHER STOWE. Crown 8vo, cloth, 10s. 6d.

Polar Expeditions. See KOLDEWEY, MARKHAM, MACGAHAN

Pottery: how it is Made, its Shape and Decoration. Practical Instructions for Painting on Porcelain and all kinds of Pottery with vitrifiable and common Oil Colours. With a full Bibliography of Standard Works upon the Ceramic Art. By G. WARD NICHOLS. 42 Illustrations, crown 8vo, red edges, 6s.

Practical (A) Handbook to the Principal Schools of England. By C. E. PASCOE. Showing the cost of living at the Great Schools, Scholarships, &c., &c. New Edition corrected to 1879, crown 8vo, cloth extra, 3s. 6d.

> "This is an exceedingly useful work, and one that was much wanted.'— *Examiner.*

Practical Treatise on Electricity and Magnetism. By J. E. H. GORDON, B.A. One volume, demy 8vo, very numerous Illustrations.

Prejevalsky (N. M.) From Kulja, across the Tian Shan to Lobnor. Translated by E. DELMAR MORGAN, F.R.G.S. With Notes and Introduction by SIR DOUGLAS FORSYTH, K.C.S.I. 1 vol., demy 8vo, with a Map.

Prince Ritto; or, The Four-leaved Shamrock. By FANNY W. CURREY. With 10 Full-page Fac-simile Reproductions of Original Drawings by HELEN O'HARA. Demy 4to, cloth extra, gilt, 10s. 6d.

Prisoner of War in Russia. See COOPE.

Publishers' Circular (The), and General Record of British and Foreign Literature. Published on the 1st and 15th of every Month.

QUARTER Sessions, from Queen Elizabeth to Queen Anne: Illustrations of Local Government and History. Drawn from Original Records (chiefly of the County of Devon). By A. H. A. HAMILTON. Crown 8vo, cloth, 10s. 6d.

RALSTON (W. R. S.) Early Russian History. Four Lectures delivered at Oxford by W. R. S. RALSTON, M.A. Crown 8vo, cloth extra, 5s.

Rambaud (Alfred). History of Russia, from its Origin to the Year 1877. With Six Maps. Translated by Mrs. L. B. LANG. 2 vols. demy 8vo, cloth extra, 38s.

> Mr. W. R. S. Ralston, in the *Academy*, says, "We gladly recognize in the present volume a trustworthy history of Russia."
> "We will venture to prophecy that it will become *the* work on the subject for readers in our part of Europe. . . . Mrs. Lang has done her work remarkably well."— *Athenæum.*

Readings in Melbourne; with an Essay on the Resources and Prospects of Victoria for the Emigrant and Uneasy Classes. By Sir ARCHIBALD MICHIE, Q.C., K.C.M.G., Agent-General for Victoria. With Coloured Map of Australia. Crown 8vo, cloth extra, price 7s. 6d.

> "Comprises more information on the prospects and resources of Victoria than any other work with which we are acquainted."—*Saturday Review.*
> "A work which is in every respect one of the most interesting and instructive that has ever been written about that land which claims to be the premier colony of the Australian group."—*The Colonies and India.*

Recollections of Samuel Breck, the American Pepys. With
Passages from his Note-Books (1771—1862). Crown 8vo, cloth, 10s. 6d.

Recollections of Writers. By CHARLES and MARY COWDEN
CLARKE. Authors of " The Concordance to Shakespeare," &c. ;
with Letters of CHARLES LAMB, LEIGH HUNT, DOUGLAS JERROLD,
and CHARLES DICKENS ; and a Preface by MARY COWDEN CLARKE.
Crown 8vo, cloth, 10s. 6d.

Reminiscences of the War in New Zealand. By THOMAS W.
GUDGEON, Lieutenant and Quartermaster, Colonial Forces, N.Z.
With Twelve Portraits. Crown 8vo, cloth extra, 10s. 6d.
    " The interest attaching at the present moment to all Britannia's ' little wars '
    should render more than ever welcome such a detailed narrative of Maori cam-
    paigns as that contained in Lieut. Gudgeon's ' Experiences of New Zealand War.' '
    —*Graphic.*

Robinson (Phil.). See " In my Indian Garden."

Rochefoucauld's Reflections. Bayard Series, 2s. 6d.

Rogers (S.) Pleasures of Memory. See " Choice Editions of
Choice Books." 2s. 6d.

Rohlfs (Dr. G.) Adventures in Morocco, and Journeys through the
Oases of Draa and Tafilet. By Dr. G. ROHLFS. Demy 8vo, Map,
and Portrait of the Author, 12s.

Rose in Bloom. See ALCOTT.

Rose Library (The). Popular Literature of all countries. Each
volume, 1s. ; cloth, 2s. 6d. Many of the Volumes are Illustrated—

1. **Sea-Gull Rock.** By JULES SANDEAU. Illustrated.
2. **Little Women.** By LOUISA M. ALCOTT.
3. **Little Women Wedded.** Forming a Sequel to "Little Women."
4. **The House on Wheels.** By MADAME DE STOLZ. Illustrated.
5. **Little Men.** By LOUISA M. ALCOTT. Dble. vol., 2s. ; cloth, 3s. 6d.
6. **The Old-Fashioned Girl.** By LOUISA M. ALCOTT. Double
   vol., 2s. ; cloth, 3s. 6d.
7. **The Mistress of the Manse.** By J. G. HOLLAND.
8. **Timothy Titcomb's Letters to Young People, Single and
   Married.**
9. **Undine, and the Two Captains.** By Baron DE LA MOTTE
   FOUQUÉ. A New Translation by F. E. BUNNETT. Illustrated.
10. **Draxy Miller's Dowry, and the Elder's Wife.** By SAXE
    HOLM.
11. **The Four Gold Pieces.** By Madame GOURAUD. Numerous
    Illustrations.
12. **Work.** A Story of Experience. First Portion. By LOUISA M.
    ALCOTT.
13. **Beginning Again.** Being a Continuation of " Work." By
    LOUISA M. ALCOTT.
14. **Picciola;** or, the Prison Flower. By X. B. SAINTINE.

The Rose Library, continued :—

15. **Robert's Holidays.** Illustrated.
16. **The Two Children of St. Domingo.** Numerous Illustrations.
17. **Aunt Jo's Scrap Bag.**
18. **Stowe (Mrs. H. B.) The Pearl of Orr's Island.**
19. ———— **The Minister's Wooing.**
20. ———— **Betty's Bright Idea.**
21. ———— **The Ghost in the Mill.**
22. ———— **Captain Kidd's Money.**
23. ———— **We and our Neighbours.** Double vol., 2*s.*
24. ———— **My Wife and I.** Double vol., 2*s.* ; cloth, gilt, 3*s.* 6*d.*
25. **Hans Brinker ; or, the Silver Skates.**
26. **Lowell's My Study Window.**
27. **Holmes (O. W.) The Guardian Angel.**
28. **Warner (C. D.) My Summer in a Garden.**
29. **Hitherto.** By the Author of "The Gayworthys." 2 vols., 1*s.* each.
30. **Helen's Babies.** By their Latest Victim.
31. **The Barton Experiment.** By the Author of "Helen's Babies."
32. **Dred.** By Mrs. BEECHER STOWE. Double vol., 2*s.* Cloth, gilt, 3*s.* 6*d.*
33. **Warner (C. D.) In the Wilderness.**
34. **Six to One.** A Seaside Story.

Russell (W. H., LL.D.) The Tour of the Prince of Wales in India, and his Visits to the Courts of Greece, Egypt, Spain, and Portugal. By W. H. RUSSELL, LL.D., who accompanied the Prince throughout his journey ; fully Illustrated by SYDNEY P. HALL, M.A., the Prince's Private Artist, with his Royal Highness's special permission to use the Sketches made during the Tour. Super-royal 8vo, cloth extra, gilt edges, 52*s.* 6*d.*; Large Paper Edition, 84*s.*

SANCTA Christina : a Story of the First Century. By ELEANOR E. ORLEBAR. With a Preface by the Bishop of Winchester. Small post 8vo, cloth extra, 5*s.*

Schweinfurth (Dr. G.) Heart of Africa. Which see.

———— *Artes Africanæ.* Illustrations and Description of Productions of the Natural Arts of Central African Tribes. With 26 Lithographed Plates, imperial 4to, boards, 28*s.*

Scientific Memoirs : being Experimental Contributions to a Knowledge of Radiant Energy. By JOHN WILLIAM DRAPER, M.D., LL.D., Author of "A Treatise on Human Physiology," &c. With Steel Portrait of the Author. Demy 8vo, cloth, 473 pages, 14*s.*

Seonee : Sporting in the Satpura Range of Central India, and in the Valley of the Nerbudda. By R. A. STERNDALE, F.R.G.S. 8vo, with numerous Illustrations, 21s.

Shakespeare (The Boudoir). Edited by HENRY CUNDELL. Carefully bracketted for reading aloud ; freed from all objectionable matter, and altogether free from notes. Price 2s. 6d. each volume, cloth extra, gilt edges. Contents :—Vol I., Cymbeline—Merchant of Venice. Each play separately, paper cover, 1s. Vol. II., As You Like It—King Lear—Much Ado about Nothing. Vol. III., Romeo and Juliet—Twelfth Night—King John. The latter six plays separately, paper cover, 9d.

Shakespeare Key (The). Forming a Companion to "The Complete Concordance to Shakespeare." By CHARLES and MARY COWDEN CLARKE. Demy 8vo, 800 pp., 21s.

Shooting : its Appliances, Practice, and Purpose. By JAMES DALZIEL DOUGALL, F.S.A., F.Z.A. Author of "Scottish Field Sports," &c. Crown 8vo, cloth extra, 10s. 6d.
"The book is admirable in every way. . . . . We wish it every success."—*Globe.*
"A very complete treatise. . . . . Likely to take high rank as an authority on shooting."—*Daily News.*

Silent Hour (The). *See* "Gentle Life Series."

Silver Pitchers. *See* ALCOTT.

Simon (Jules). *See* "Government of M. Thiers."

Six to One. A Seaside Story. 16mo, boards, 1s.

Sketches from an Artist's Portfolio. By SYDNEY P. HALL. About 60 Fac-similes of his Sketches during Travels in various parts of Europe. Folio, cloth extra, 3l. 3s.
"A portfolio which any one might be glad to call their own."—*Times.*

Sleepy Sketches ; or, How we Live, and How we Do Not Live. From Bombay. 1 vol., small post 8vo, cloth, 6s.
"Well-written and amusing sketches of Indian society."—*Morning Post.*

Smith (G.) Assyrian Explorations and Discoveries. By the late GEORGE SMITH. Illustrated by Photographs and Woodcuts. Demy 8vo, 6th Edition, 18s.

———— *The Chaldean Account of Genesis.* Containing the Description of the Creation, the Fall of Man, the Deluge, the Tower of Babel, the Times of the Patriarchs, and Nimrod ; Babylonian Fables, and Legends of the Gods ; from the Cuneiform Inscriptions. By the late G. SMITH, of the Department of Oriental Antiquities, British Museum. With many Illustrations. Demy 8vo, cloth extra, 5th Edition, 16s.

Snow-Shoes and Canoes ; or, the Adventures of a Fur-Hunter in the Hudson's Bay Territory. By W. H. G. KINGSTON. 2nd Edition. With numerous Illustrations. Square crown 8vo, cloth extra, gilt, 7s. 6d.

South Australia: its History, Resources, and Productions.
Edited by W. HARCUS, J.P., with 66 full-page Woodcut Illustrations
from Photographs taken in the Colony, and 2 Maps. Demy 8vo, 21s.

Spain. Illustrated by GUSTAVE DORÉ. Text by the BARON
CH. D'AVILLIER. Containing over 240 Wood Engravings by DORÉ,
half of them being Full-page size. Imperial 4to, elaborately bound
in cloth, extra gilt edges, 3l. 3s.

Stanley (H. M.) How I Found Livingstone. Crown 8vo, cloth
extra, 7s. 6d. ; large Paper Edition, 10s. 6d.

———— *"My Kalulu," Prince, King, and Slave.* A Story
from Central Africa. Crown 8vo, about 430 pp., with numerous graphic
Illustrations, after Original Designs by the Author. Cloth, 7s. 6d.

———— *Coomassie and Magdala.* A Story of Two British
Campaigns in Africa. Demy 8vo, with Maps and Illustrations, 16s.

———— *Through the Dark Continent,* which see.

St. Nicholas for 1879. 1s. monthly.

Story without an End. From the German of Carové, by the late
Mrs. SARAH T. AUSTIN. Crown 4to, with 15 Exquisite Drawings
by E. V. B., printed in Colours in Fac-simile of the original Water
Colours ; and numerous other Illustrations. New Edition, 7s. 6d.

———— square 4to, with Illustrations by HARVEY. 2s. 6d.

Stowe (Mrs. Beecher) Dred. Cheap Edition, boards, 2s. Cloth,
gilt edges, 3s. 6d.

———— *Footsteps of the Master.* With Illustrations and red
borders. Small post 8vo, cloth extra, 6s.

———— *Geography,* with 60 Illustrations. Square cloth, 4s. 6d.

———— *Little Foxes.* Cheap Edition, 1s. ; Library Edition,
4s. 6d.

———— *Betty's Bright Idea.* 1s.

———— *My Wife and I ; or, Harry Henderson's History.*
Small post 8vo, cloth extra, 6s.*

———— *Minister's Wooing,* 5s.; Copyright Series, 1s. 6d.; cl., 2s.*

———— *Old Town Folk.* 6s. : Cheap Edition, 2s. 6d.

———— *Old Town Fireside Stories.* Cloth extra, 3s. 6d.

———— *Our Folks at Poganuc.* 10s. 6d.

———— *We and our Neighbours.* 1 vol., small post 8vo, 6s.
Sequel to "My Wife and I."*

———— *Pink and White Tyranny.* Small post 8vo, 3s. 6d. ;
Cheap Edition, 1s. 6d. and 2s.

———— *Queer Little People.* 1s. ; cloth, 2s.

———— *Chimney Corner.* 1s. ; cloth, 1s. 6d.

———— *The Pearl of Orr's Island.* Crown 8vo, 5s.*

Stowe (Mrs. Beecher) Little Pussey Willow. Fcap., 2s.

——— *Woman in Sacred History.* Illustrated with 15 Chromo-lithographs and about 200 pages of Letterpress. Demy 4to, cloth extra, gilt edges, 25s.

Street Life in London. By J. THOMSON, F.R.G.S., and ADOLPHE SMITH. One volume, 4to, containing 40 Permanent Photographs of Scenes of London Street Life, with Descriptive Letterpress, 25s.

Student's French Examiner. By F. JULIEN, Author of "Petites Leçons de Conversation et de Grammaire." Square crown 8vo, cloth extra, 2s.

Studies from Nature. 24 Photographs, with Descriptive Letter-press. By STEVEN THOMPSON. Imperial 4to, 35s.

Sub-Tropical Rambles. See PIKE (N).

Sullivan (A. M., M.P.). See "New Ireland."

Sulphuric Acid (A Practical Treatise on the Manufacture of). By A. G. and C. G. LOCK, Consulting Chemical Engineers. With 77 Construction Plates, drawn to scale measurements, and other Illustrations.

Summer Holiday in Scandinavia (A). By E. L. L. ARNOLD. Crown 8vo, cloth extra, 10s. 6d.

Sumner (Hon. Charles). See Life and Letters.

Surgeon's Handbook on the Treatment of Wounded in War. By Dr. FRIEDRICH ESMARCH, Professor of Surgery in the University of Kiel, and Surgeon-General to the Prussian Army. Translated by H. H. CLUTTON, B.A. Cantab, F.R.C.S. Numerous Coloured Plates and Illustrations, 8vo, strongly bound in flexible leather, 1l. 8s.

TAUCHNITZ'S English Editions of German Authors. Each volume, cloth flexible, 2s. ; or sewed, 1s. 6d. (Catalogues post free on application.)

——— *(B.) German and English Dictionary.* Cloth, 1s. 6d.; roan, 2s.

——— *French and English.* Paper, 1s. 6d. ; cloth, 2s ; roan, 2s. 6d.

——— *Italian and English.* Paper, 1s. 6d. ; cloth, 2s. ; roan, 2s. 6d.

——— *Spanish and English.* Paper, 1s. 6d. ; cloth, 2s. ; roan, 2s. 6d.

——— *New Testament.* Cloth, 2s. ; gilt, 2s. 6d.

The Telephone. An Account of the Phenomena of Electricity, Magnetism, and Sound. By Prof. A. E. DOLBEAR, Author of "The Art of Projecting," &c. Second Edition, with an Appendix Descriptive of Prof. BELL's Present Instrument. 130 pp., with 19 Illus-

Tennyson's May Queen. Choicely Illustrated from designs by the Hon. Mrs. BOYLE. Crown 8vo (*See* Choice Series), 2*s.* 6*d.*

Textbook (A) of Harmony. For the Use of Schools and Students. By the late CHARLES EDWARD HORSLEY. Revised for the Press by WESTLEY RICHARDS and W. H. CALCOTT. Small post 8vo, cloth extra, 3*s.* 6*d.*

Thebes, and its Five Greater Temples. See ABNEY.

Thirty Short Addresses for Family Prayers or Cottage Meetings. By "FIDELIS." Author of "Simple Preparation for the Holy Communion." Containing Addresses by the late Canon Kingsley, Rev. G. H. Wilkinson, and Dr. Vaughan. Crown 8vo, cloth extra, 5*s.*

Thomson (J.) The Straits of Malacca, Indo-China, and China ; or, Ten Years' Travels, Adventures, and Residence Abroad. By J. THOMSON, F.R.G.S., Author of "Illustrations of China and its People." Upwards of 60 Woodcuts. Demy 8vo, cloth extra, 21*s.*

—————— *Through Cyprus with the Camera, in the Autumn of* 1878. Sixty large and very fine Permanent Photographs, illustrating the Coast and Inland Scenery of Cyprus, and the Costumes and Types of the Natives, specially taken on a journey undertaken for the purpose. By JOHN THOMSON, F.R.G.S., Author of "Illustrations of China and its People," &c. Two royal 4to volumes, cloth extra, 105*s.*

Thorne (E.) The Queen of the Colonies ; or, Queensland as I saw it. 1 vol., with Map, 6*s.*

Through the Dark Continent : The Sources of the Nile ; Around the Great Lakes, and down the Congo. By HENRY M. STANLEY. 2 vols., demy 8vo, containing 150 Full-page and other Illustrations, 2 Portraits of the Author, and 10 Maps, 42*s.* Sixth Thousand.

—————— *(Map to the above).* Size 34 by 56 inches, showing, on a large scale, Stanley's recent Great Discoveries in Central Africa. The First Map in which the Congo was ever correctly traced. Mounted, in case, 1*l.* 1*s.*

"One of the greatest geographical discoveries of the age."—*Spectator.*

"Mr. Stanley has penetrated the very heart of the mystery. . . . He has opened up a perfectly virgin region, never before, so far as known, visited by a white man."—*Times.*

To the Arctic Regions and Back in Six Weeks. By Captain A. W. M. CLARK KENNEDY (late of the Coldstream Guards). With Illustrations and Maps. 8vo, cloth, 15*s.*

Tour of the Prince of Wales in India. See RUSSELL.

Trees and Ferns. By F. G. HEATH. Crown 8vo, cloth, gilt edges, with numerous Illustrations, 3*s.* 6*d.*

Turkistan. Notes of a Journey in the Russian Provinces of Central Asia and the Khanates of Bokhara and Kokand. By EUGENE SCHUYLER, Secretary to the American Legation, St. Petersburg. Numerous Illustrations. 2 vols, 8vo, cloth extra, 5th Edition, 2*l.* 2*s.*

Two Americas ; being an Account of Sport and Travel, with Notes on Men and Manners in North and South America. By Sir ROSE PRICE, Bart. 1 vol., demy 8vo, with Illustrations, cloth extra, 2nd Edition, 18*s.*

Two Friends. By LUCIEN BIART, Author of "Adventures of a Young Naturalist," "My Rambles in the New World," &c. Small post 8vo, numerous Illustrations, 7*s.* 6*d.*

Two Supercargoes (The) ; or, Adventures in Savage Africa. By W. H. G. KINGSTON. Square imperial 16mo, cloth extra, 7*s.* 6*d.* Numerous Full-page Illustrations.

VANDENHOFF (George, M.A.). See "Art of Reading Aloud."

———— *Clerical Assistant.* Fcap., 3*s.* 6*d.*

———— *Ladies' Reader (The).* Fcap., 5*s.*

Verne's (Jules) Works. Translated from the French, with from 50 to 100 Illustrations. Each cloth extra, gilt edges—

Large post 8vo, price 10*s.* 6*d. each*—
1. **Fur Country.** Plainer binding, cloth, 5*s.*
2. **Twenty Thousand Leagues under the Sea.**
3. **From the Earth to the Moon, and a Trip round It.** Plainer binding, cloth, 5*s.*
4. **Michael Strogoff, the Courier of the Czar.**
5. **Hector Servadac.**
6. **Dick Sands, the Boy Captain.**

Imperial 16*mo, price* 7*s.* 6*d. each.* *Those marked with* * *in plainer cloth binding,* 3*s.* 6*d. each.*
1. **Five Weeks in a Balloon.**
2. **Adventures of Three Englishmen and Three Russians in South Africa.**
3. ***Around the World in Eighty Days.**
4. **A Floating City, and the Blockade Runners.**
5. ***Dr. Ox's Experiment, Master Zacharius, A Drama in the Air, A Winter amid the Ice, &c.**
6. **The Survivors of the "Chancellor."**
7. ***Dropped from the Clouds.** } The **Mysterious Island.** 3 vols.,
8. ***Abandoned.** 22*s.* 6*d.* One volume, with some of the
9. ***Secret of the Island.** } Illustrations, cloth, gilt edges, 10*s.* 6*d.*
10. **The Child of the Cavern.**

The following Cheaper Editions are issued with a few of the Illustrations, in paper wrapper, price 1*s. ; cloth gilt,* 2*s. each.*
1. **Adventures of Three Englishmen and Three Russians in South Africa.**
2. **Five Weeks in a Balloon.**

Verne's (Jules) Works, continued :—

3. A Floating City.
4. The Blockade Runners.
5. From the Earth to the Moon.
6. Around the Moon.
7. Twenty Thousand Leagues under the Sea. Vol. I.
8. ———— Vol. II. The two parts in one, cloth, gilt, 3s. 6d.
9. Around the World in Eighty Days.
10. Dr. Ox's Experiment, and Master Zacharius.
11. Martin Paz, the Indian Patriot.
12. A Winter amid the Ice.
13. The Fur Country. Vol. I.
14. ———— Vol. II. Both parts in one, cloth gilt, 3s. 6d.
15. Survivors of the "Chancellor." Vol. I.
16. ———— Vol. II. Both volumes in one, cloth, gilt edges, 3s. 6d.

Viardot (Louis). See "Painters of all Schools."

Visit to the Court of Morocco. By A. LEARED, Author of "Morocco and the Moors." Map and Illustrations, 8vo, 5s.

W*ALLER (Rev. C. H.) The Names on the Gates of Pearl,* and other Studies. By the Rev. C. H. WALLER, M.A. Second edition. Crown 8vo, cloth extra, 6s.

———— *A Grammar and Analytical Vocabulary of the Words in* the Greek Testament. Compiled from Brüder's Concordance. For the use of Divinity Students and Greek Testament Classes. By the Rev. C. H. WALLER, M.A., late Scholar of University College, Oxford, Tutor of the London College of Divinity, St. John's Hall, Highbury. Part I., The Grammar. Small post 8vo, cloth, 2s. 6d. Part II. The Vocabulary, 2s. 6d.

———— *Adoption and the Covenant.* Some Thoughts on Confirmation. Super-royal 16mo, cloth limp, 2s. 6d.

War in Bulgaria: a Narrative of Personal Experiences. By LIEUTENANT-GENERAL VALENTINE BAKER PASHA. Maps and Plans of Battles. 2 vols., demy 8vo, cloth extra, 2l. 2s.

Warner (C. D.) My Summer in a Garden. Rose Library, 1s.

———— *Back-log Studies.* Boards, 1s. 6d. ; cloth, 2s.

———— *In the Wilderness.* Rose Library, 1s.

———— *Mummies and Moslems.* 8vo, cloth, 12s.

Weaving. See "History and Principles."

Whitney (Mrs. A. D. T.) The Gayworthys. Cloth, 3s. 6d.

———— *Faith Gartney.* Small post 8vo, 3s. 6d. Cheaper Editions, 1s. 6d. and 2s.

———— *Real Folks.* 12mo, crown, 3s. 6d.

Whitney (Mrs. A. D. T.) Hitherto. Small post 8vo, 3s. 6d. and 2s. 6d.

——— *Sights and Insights.* 3 vols., crown 8vo, 31s. 6d.

———— *Summer in Leslie Goldthwaite's Life.* Cloth, 3s. 6d.

———— *The Other Girls.* Small post 8vo, cloth extra, 3s. 6d.

——— *We Girls.* Small post 8vo, 3s. 6d.; Cheap Edition, 1s. 6d. and 2s.

Wikoff (H.) The Four Civilizations of the World. An Historical Retrospect. Crown 8vo, cloth, 12s.

Wills, A Few Hints on Proving, without Professional Assistance. By a PROBATE COURT OFFICIAL. 5th Edition, revised with Forms of Wills, Residuary Accounts, &c. Fcap. 8vo, cloth limp, 1s.

With Axe and Rifle on the Western Prairies. By W. H. G. KINGSTON. With numerous Illustrations, square crown 8vo, cloth extra, gilt, 7s. 6d.

Woolsey (C. D., LL.D.) Introduction to the Study of International Law; designed as an Aid in Teaching and in Historical Studies. 5th Edition, demy 8vo, 18s.

Words of Wellington: Maxims and Opinions, Sentences and Reflections of the Great Duke, gathered from his Despatches, Letters, and Speeches (Bayard Series). 2s. 6d.

World of Comets. By A. GUILLEMIN, Author of "The Heavens." Translated and edited by JAMES GLAISHER, F.R.S. 1 vol., super-royal 8vo, with numerous Woodcut Illustrations, and 3 Chromo-lithographs, cloth extra, 31s. 6d.

"The mass of information collected in the volume is immense, and the treatment of the subject is so purely popular, that none need be deterred from a perusal of it."—*British Quarterly Review.*

Wreck of the Grosvenor. By W. CLARK RUSSELL. 6s. Third and Cheaper Edition.

XENOPHON'S Anabasis; or, Expedition of Cyrus. A Literal Translation, chiefly from the Text of Dindorff, by GEORGE B. WHEELER. Books I to III. Crown 8vo, boards, 2s.

——— *Books I. to VII.* Boards, 3s. 6d.

www.ingramcontent.com/pod-product-compliance
Lightning Source LLC
Chambersburg PA
CBHW020619030726
47497CB00007B/2312